———————————— ★ ————————————

The fire had run straight up from the curtains and furniture below. The floor was gone and the walls had been reduced to charred timbers. There really wasn't much to see, and Karl handed me a couple of color photos from his packet. They showed an elegant and richly appointed room with what looked to be an antique bed, some beautiful mirrors, and several hundred yards of silk drapery material. "An arsonist's dream."

"She didn't have a chance," Karl agreed.

"And if she'd been able-bodied?"

"Awake and alert instantly—maybe. Asleep, not a prayer. By the time she'd have waked up, it would have been too late even if she'd been a champion sprinter. It was that fast."

———————————— ★ ————————————

Also available from Worldwide Mystery by
JANICE LAW

A SAFE PLACE TO DIE

JANICE LAW

BACKFIRE

WORLDWIDE.

TORONTO • NEW YORK • LONDON
AMSTERDAM • PARIS • SYDNEY • HAMBURG
STOCKHOLM • ATHENS • TOKYO • MILAN
MADRID • WARSAW • BUDAPEST • AUCKLAND

BACKFIRE

A Worldwide Mystery/May 1996

First published by St. Martin's Press, Incorporated.

ISBN 0-373-26201-9

Printed in U.S.A.

To Duncan and Elizabeth Murray

ONE

Sticky subtropical weather hung on over D.C. that September, a fit accompaniment for the wrangles on the Hill and the hesitations in the White House. We'd spent all spring diverted by the fumbles of the Democrats and the malice of the Republicans. Now, however, we'd had almost enough of the peccadilloes of the rich and electable. Bored and heat-struck, the high brackets bitched about taxes, the middle brackets fretted about health care, and the poor stood about on the street corners and declared nothing much had changed.

Actually, politics may not change, but the personnel does. And fresh faces, confronted with D.C. crime stats and the fever of self-importance that rises from the Potomac, find their way to Executive Security. The newly elected and the lucky appointed want assistants vetted, offices swept for bugs, and new security systems installed in their rented Georgetown houses.

Our political clients run to pressured self-importance, so the concise and cryptic little note that rolled out of our office fax that Monday morning was something of a novelty. The message accurately quoted Executive Security's standard rates, solicited my efforts for one Maria Rivas, and promised a bank check within the day.

The name of my prospective client did not ring any bells; there was neither name nor return address, and the phone number of the originating message proved to be a small stationery shop that had a fax machine and a copier on the premises. I asked Martha, my secretary, to keep an eye out for the check and returned to our main task of the moment, tracking down the well-hidden assets of a spectacularly bankrupt developer.

At 12:45 the same day, a check arrived, all very official, drawn on a large local D.C. bank for the specified sum. The check had been signed by one of the bank officials and, in place of the remitter's name, there was a notation "for Maria Rivas defense" in green ink. I had Martha put it in our safe and tried to think if I had ever heard of Maria Rivas. At 3:00 p.m., just back from lunch with a foreign embassy official who suspected his quarters of being bugged, I got the first call. Martha buzzed my line and said, "Funny phone call."

I picked up. "Anna Peters. Can I help you?"

"Has the check arrived?" The voice was oddly hollow and metallic, intelligible, but distorted enough to make recognition impossible.

"The check for Maria Rivas? Yes, it has, Mr. . . . ."

"Mr. Smith will do."

"It would be helpful, Mr. Smith, if you could tell me something more about the situation."

"You've heard of the Skane arson case?"

I had, of course. D.C. has a high crime rate, and blasé residents tend to be more taken with political than with criminal bloodletting. The thoroughly nasty Skane case had proved an exception, mesmerizing the public ever since the wealthy developer-restaurateur's showcase home had burned to the ground.

Lost in the fire had been Mrs. Skane, a longtime invalid confined to a wheelchair. A gas can recovered on the property pointed to arson, and the trail led to the au pair who'd been minding the Skane grandchildren during the summer holidays. It suddenly struck me that though we'd had a veritable banquet of Skanes—Skane family, Skane restaurants, Skane opulence, Skane charities—we'd been told very little about the supposed perpetrator.

"Maria Rivas—was that the name of the young woman accused of setting the fire?"

"That's right." My informant gurgled like Darth Vader.

"Where is she now?"

"She is in custody." He mentioned one of D.C.'s plusher suburbs.

"She hasn't been able to make bail?"

"No. She has been under treatment—for shock."

"I see. Who's handling her defense?"

"Lauren Emby."

"What firm is that?" I asked as I wrote the name on my pad.

"He's a public defender."

This was unusual. We do handle some pro bono work for the local Legal Aid Services—the consequence of an unguarded moment of philanthropic sentiment—but most of that has proved to be routine: tracing witnesses and deadbeat fathers, double-checking state's evidence, providing expert advice about minor fires, and undertaking an occasional surveillance job. Such good works have proved to be a fine way to break in new trainees as well as providing entrée to a variety of neighborhoods remote from Executive Security's usual corporate environs. A high-profile arson-murder case was definitely not in our garden-variety pro bono line.

"Of course, I expect to pay you," my caller said. "If the retainer is not sufficient . . ."

"The retainer is perfectly adequate, thank you. But if you are interested in Ms. Rivas's defense, you might do better to invest the money in a topflight lawyer. A big firm that handles criminal cases has resources even the most competent public defender can't match. You can always get investigative services if her lawyer thinks they're really necessary."

The metallic voice cut me off. "I'm not interested in lawyers. Will you take the case?"

The smart answer, of course, was no. Mysterious fax transmissions, voice-distortion devices, and an anonymous interest in a high-profile case are not the recipe for business tranquillity. On the other hand, I knew what it was like to be a young woman without money in the vicinity of great wealth.

"I'd want to meet with Maria Rivas before I decide," I said.

I made a few notes, then went to look for Rosita Guzman, an intern who was another consequence of the same burst of goodwill that had brought us pro bono work. Rosita had been on the job for two months, and her fluent Spanish had already made her valuable to our Legal Aid connections and occasionally useful to us.

I went downstairs to the cramped little office that we've set up for the interns in a former storage room. If my husband wasn't part owner of our present building, Executive Security would probably have moved to larger quarters a couple of years ago. We stayed when Harry's Helios Workshop went through some tough financial times at the end of the eighties and needed our rent. There is some advantage to keeping business in the family.

Rosita had the door open to get a little light from the hall windows, and Mike Garrett was standing in the doorway, speaking to her in his perfectly fluent Spanish. In English, Mike is gruff, businesslike, almost curt. In Spanish, he is elaborate, polite, almost courtly. It may be true after all that to learn another language is to acquire another soul.

But then Mike Garrett is a curious man with a curious past. He had been a bodyguard both in the States and in Latin America before he came to work for me almost a decade ago. Right from the first, I'd been struck by his obvious intelligence and competence and puzzled by his choice of a profession better known for brawn than brains. It took me a good deal of time to convince him to accept any supervisory or administrative functions, and although he's an excellent worker and a good colleague, he always becomes restless if he's kept inside the office too long.

"Hi, Mike. How are you doing, Rosita?"

"Very well, thank you, Anna."

"She's made a kill," Mike said.

Rosita beamed. "I've found Simon Delgado."

It took me a minute to remember that Delgado was her first project, a fly-by-night used-car dealer who had quit paying alimony and child support to his wife and seven children. "Bravo! And has he any assets?"

"You bet. A big car lot in San Diego. The Police out there say he was in the process of liquidating the business."

"And let me guess—decamping to Mexico?"

"Right." She looked at her computer screen with satisfaction. "I didn't think it would be such a thrill."

"There's nothing like it," I agreed. Though I find myself complaining about the expense of our pro bono work and the time involved with our interns, I secretly enjoy turning out investigators. I understand now the pleasure that old Brahmin, my teacher at New World Oil, took in my education. Rosita and any successors are my thanks to him.

"And this on the computer, no less," Mike said. Mike is like me. He likes to get out, see the sites, sniff the air, so to speak. Rosita is of the new computer generation.

She patted the machine affectionately. "The Social Security number came right up on the screen and I knew we'd found him."

"And this is your final report for—I forget who you're working with...."

"Laura Sutherland."

"Oh, right. Laura'll be pleased."

"Totally."

Mike repeated his congratulations and left, and I asked Rosita whether she knew a Lauren Emby.

She looked up, pushing back her untidy black hair, her round face earnest and alert. Rosita is a pleasure to have in the office; she's ambitious and enthusiastic without the heartlessness one sometimes sees in the career-minded.

"Emby? I think I know who he is, but I haven't met him. Small African-American, wears lovely suits. I've seen him around the court. He's supposed to be good. Everyone says he won't be a public defender long."

Not if he gets Ms. Rivas off, I thought. The Skane case had touched a nerve among the privileged classes and sent shock waves through the pricey urban enclaves and fancy suburbs. Suddenly, the normally anonymous army of immigrant cleaners, housekeepers, child-minders, cooks, and gardeners—so reliable, so willing, so cheap—took on a sinister hue. Servants who had been a convenience now seemed a threat, and all over the Beltway, folks woke up to find that they'd been leaving their nearest and dearest with strangers.

There was an element of hysteria—and guilt—in all this. With unseemly haste, even our better papers declared the case open and shut, passing over the accused with averted eyes to concentrate on the undeniable tragedy for the Skane family and on the dangers posed by ill-screened domestics.

Upstairs, after I put Martha to work rounding up everything she could find in the back newspapers about the Skane family and the fire, I got on the phone.

When I finally connected with Emby just before 4:30, he sounded tired and harassed.

"Mr. Smith, huh?" he said when I explained about Ms. Rivas's mysterious benefactor.

"Mr. Smith and a voice-distortion device, too."

"I think he's wasting his money and your time," Emby said.

"As bad as that?"

"As far as evidence goes. I got half a dozen cases I could use an investigator on, but this one..."

I mentioned our connection to Legal Aid, and Emby said he'd keep it in mind.

"So," I said, "can we get together? I might as well take a look at what you've got."

He sighed and I heard the ruffling of pages. He was going to be in court the next three days.

"What time do you have to be there?"

"Not before ten. I could see you at nine tomorrow or Wednesday, if you don't mind meeting at the courthouse."

"That's fine," I said. "I'll need authorization to see Maria Rivas and whatever you've been given in the way of evidence. The more the better."

He gave a short cynical laugh. "You may not think so when you see the brief."

A SMOGGY MIST cloaked the Potomac, slowing traffic all the way out to the Skanes' suburb. The boxy red brick courthouse was already half-filled when I arrived: worried looking women with noisy children; lost young men with uneasy eyes and unsteady gaits; a few swaggering toughs; a number of hard-pressed small businessmen caught on the wrong side of the law; a few matriarchs, massive, skeptical, and sad; and a sprinkling of middle-class traffic offenders and DWI cases. These were all small-timers; the supposedly dangerous were sequestered elsewhere, to be trotted out in prison garb when their moment to answer came.

I looked around the crowd of briefcase- and clipboard-toting lawyers before I found one who matched Rosita's description: a slim brown-skinned man whose elegantly cut gray summer suit stood out from the mass of drip-dry and polyester.

"Lauren Emby?"

He shook my hand and glanced around. "I'm not sure there's a room free," he said.

"We could stand outside if you want. The heat's not as bad as it's going to be."

"This won't take long," he said. "A minute, please, I'll be right back, Mrs. Greene. No, nothing new," he told another imploring client. "I've told you that."

He took a deep breath of the cloying air outside and shook his head.

"I take it you're hardly looking for work."

"Let's just say the government is getting its money's worth." He handed over a fat manila envelope. "I had the office make you copies of everything we've got. I called the jail and said you'd be coming by, that you were working with us."

"Fine. Do you have time to tell me anything about the case, about our client, or about the Skanes?"

He hesitated only a minute. He looked as if fatigue was a chronic condition, and after the briefest of looks back at the crowded lobby and his doubtless importunate clients, he nodded. "Nothing much I'm going to change in there, anyway. Well, then, the case. I'd prefer you met our client without any preconceptions. Your impressions might be a help to me."

"Fair enough. I'm planning to stop there today. What about the rest of the Skane household?"

"Households," he said. "There are three large houses in the compound, a guest house, and what amounts to a small apartment house over the garage."

"All the cars are in one garage?"

"For all three families. It sits toward the back of the property."

"You'd think that would have been inconvenient."

"Phone system," Lauren said. "They had someone on call at all hours to bring cars round."

"How the other half lives."

"You said it. The main house held Joseph and Helena Skane; our client, Maria Rivas; the cook, Molly Portman, and her husband, Peter, the butler; also Antonia and Luisa Ceasario, who did the laundry, helped in the kitchen, and generally did the unskilled housework. The Portmans had an apartment on the lower level of the main building. The Ceasarios have rooms over the garage."

"And Maria?"

"She had a room on the third floor, down the hall from Mrs. Skane's bedroom."

"Really?"

"When you see the size of the house, you'll realize they were acres apart. Now the rest of the family. Tony Skane lives in the large brick house on the right side of the property. He's getting married soon. His sister, Sabrina, and her husband, Arnold Bach, live in the similar house on the left. They have two children—two and four, I think."

"Staff in both houses?"

"Oh yes. Cook-housekeepers with extra day help. Professional cleaning firm comes in once a week and does the whole compound top to bottom."

"Anyone outside, or did they use a lawn service?"

"Lawn service—Green and Gro—but they did have a full-time chauffeur who ferried the kids around and maintained the cars. And there's a gardener. Mrs. Skane was fond of flowers. They had a man to run the greenhouse on the property."

"Longtime staff?"

"Some. The Portmans seem to have been around a long time. The chauffeur was fairly new—couple of years. The kids' staffs were all recent, as were the Ceasarios."

"And we know where all these people were the night of the fire?"

"Yes. Both Tony Skane and the Bachs were out at the same party, a big political fund-raiser that Joseph Skane also attended. The grandchildren were visiting their mother's family in Arlington for the weekend. The staff had gotten the night off, except for the Portmans and John Delano, the chauffeur, who were on call in case Mrs. Skane wanted anything. The Portmans, however, also wanted to go out—their daughter's birthday or something—and Maria volunteered to stay in with Mrs. Skane.''

''And I suppose they all have alibis?''

''Yes. The Portmans were at their daughter's house with several of her neighbors. The chauffeur's a computer buff, and I'm told that he was on a computer net all evening. The police took a good look at him, but his computer log collaborates his statement and there was absolutely no physical evidence to make him suspect.''

''Moving on to the family,'' I said.

''They were all seen at the fund-raising dinner and dance. In fact, the party was videotaped. Joseph Skane was one of the speakers and sat at the head table. No doubt he was there the whole time. The others are visible in the crowd in some of the background shots.''

''I'm interested in Joseph Skane. The papers say he and Maria Rivas were lovers. Any proof of that?''

''Just his word.''

''And what's he like?''

''Now, that is the bonus question,'' Lauren said. ''I can give you either the official line or my gut feelings.''

''Better give me both.''

''Officially, he's a successful restaurateur turned developer, one of the richest men in the state. He kept his shirt on in the eighties and has been buying out the bankrupts at fire-sale prices. The cash comes from his restaurant chain—make that chains. He also owns a down-market string of family-type restaurants.''

"That's in addition to the Beefeaters? Is that what I read?"

"Yeah, that's right, Beefeaters. Megabucks."

"So I understand."

"Fiscal genius in any case. He's selling himself on having had the smarts to avoid the crash."

"He's into HUD, though. Didn't his firm have something to do with that D.C. tower project there's been the flap over?"

"It did indeed. He has his fingers in a number of other interesting buildings, too. He's very well connected."

"Any more good news?"

"Read the papers: He's a pillar of the community, a devoted husband, an admirable father and stepfather."

"Stepfather?"

"The daughter is his wife's by her first marriage. The boy is his."

"And it was the stepdaughter's children that Maria was hired to supervise?"

"Not exactly. Maria, as far as I understand, was hired for Mrs. Skane. She was a trained nurse back in Guatemala. Hasn't been able to pass the language exam here yet. The business with the kids was a strictly temporary measure. Maria agreed to help with the baby-sitting until they found a replacement nanny."

"Which is why she remained in her room in the senior Skanes' house?"

"I imagine. Of course, they all lived together in what is always referred to as 'the Skane family compound.'"

"A close family, then?"

"So they say."

"The wife . . ."

"Helena."

"Helena was asleep at the time of the fire?"

"That's correct."

"What time was that?"

"The police and the fire marshal estimate it started around ten p.m."

"An early bedtime."

"Skane says his wife was a semi-invalid, which was one reason for the children living on the property."

"Skane says?"

"No very clear diagnosis—some vague back injury. Of course there wasn't much left for the autopsy."

"But no sign of foul play?"

"Just the fact that someone torched the house and let her burn to death."

I HAD ARRANGED to see Maria Rivas around midday, and after I concluded my interview with Lauren Emby, I decided to have a look at the remains of the Skanes' suburban home. It was several miles away from the county court geographically and several thousand miles away in ambience. The compound was located in a vintage mid-eighties luxury development with a winding system of roads and wooded lots so large that the houses were virtually invisible from the street. I took some time to find the right entrance, and when I did find it, I was surprised by the building that loomed at the end of the long curving drive.

Even minus the damaged center section, the house was enormous, a vast, ungainly expanse of glass facades and pretentious colonnades facing a man-made pond complete with little sluiceways and bridges and several acres of well-barbered shrubs. It looked more like corporate headquarters than home sweet home. Still, as edifice mania goes, this was impressive, and so was the efficiency of the security guard who bustled up, ready with exhortations about the sanctity of property and privacy. I handed over my credentials and got out of the car.

"You'll have to make arrangements to see the interior," the guard said, returning my authorization. He was pale, plump, and well on the far side of middle age. "No way I can do that."

"Today I just wanted to see the layout and the damage."

"You'll see that best from the rear of the house," he said. Now that I was kosher, he was prepared to be friendly. I guessed that he found tramping around the Skane château a tiresome beat. He helpfully pointed out details of the house, such as the driveway that had run under the portico to the open court beyond. Since that was closed off now with plywood barricades, he led me around the side, and past the acre or so of glass, marble, and steel that comprised the building.

"Square footage?" the guard said in answer to my question. "Oh, I'd say getting on to thirty thousand square feet. That's the main building."

"A tidy little property."

"Kept adding on was what I'd heard. Whatever he saw, he wanted—that type. And then they'd call in the builders for an addition; you know how it is."

"It looks like a hotel. I'm surprised the neighbors didn't complain."

"Well, you can always complain," the guard observed. "Doesn't mean anything's done, does it?"

"It couldn't have been torched by a disgruntled neighbor, could it?"

"Not much chance of that," the guard said with a laugh. "That foreign gal did it. Though I'd guess more than one has thought about it."

"Lots of girlfriends?"

"I used to work the parties. I can tell you," he said, "the guy knows how to throw a party."

We had reached the corner of the building. Another stretch of glass revealed an indoor swimming pool and an exercise salon.

"Bowling alley, too," the guard said. "Sauna, squash court, an indoor tennis court, firing range down in the basement. All this here's the entertainment area." He waved his hand expansively.

"I'd have thought they'd have gotten enough exercise just walking around the place."

"Not much for walking, any of them. Mr. Skane had a golf cart—two or three, in fact. Used them for golf and tooled around the place in them. Sometimes after parties, we'd have to fish them out of the ponds.''

"So your company's worked for the Skanes quite some time?''

"Since they put up the house. What would that be—1985, maybe? Think so. Got stiffed on the house, though. They'll never get what it cost them. See that." The guard pointed. "See that rust streak? That's coming from the steelwork. That means a leak somewhere. Same all through—cracks in the concrete, marble panels coming loose. Yes, the contractor stiffed him." He spoke with a contained relish.

"And you think they'll sell the house now?" I asked as we descended a considerable grade. Through a pretty grove of Japanese maples, I could see the lawn and the big circular gravel drive that ran in front of the two smaller Skane houses. Both were oversized brick jobs but considerably more conventional in design than the main building. Farther back was a large vinyl-sided garage: The Skanes had not had much concept of unified design.

"Dunno. I wouldn't want to live in it," the guard said. "They'll never get that burned smell out. And you see, the whole center section was destroyed: the living rooms, the main bedrooms, the dining room, the kitchen. The guts of the place are gone.''

From the front, the house hadn't looked too bad—blackened walls and boarded-up windows. The back revealed twisted girders, shattered blocks of concrete, and dislodged slabs of marble: a gaping ruin with all the peculiar shabbiness of modern synthetics in disaster.

"It looks like it was hit by a bomb, don't it?"

"Indeed," I said. In fact, a bomb would be the nearest equivalent. Once a fire gets started in a building with an atrium, the open area acts like a chimney. When enough of a fire builds up, it literally explodes into the adjoining rooms. I've watched a demonstration at the fire-safety lab, and it's damn impressive.

"We saw it the next day," our guide added. "Still hot. There—that was the master bedroom."

I looked up at the remains: a spaghetti of wires, charred boards, and reinforcing steel. Behind us were woods and a garden visible beyond the buildings. Another pond, complete with swans, lay to our right. The Skanes' bedroom must have had a lovely view; the walls, as in the other rooms, had been mostly glass. Central air conditioning, of course, climate-controlled, doubtless computer-monitored; the room had been three stories up, opening on an atrium, with sealed exterior windows: the very latest in modern comfort and convenience—and a deathtrap.

"Did you see much of Mrs. Skane?"

"Sure. They entertained a lot."

"She was in a wheelchair?"

"Yes and no. She could walk. I've seen her walk. Walk around at a cocktail party, come by, you know, and check that everything was all right."

That was interesting.

"When she got tired, she'd call for the chair. Back injury, she told me one night."

"Any idea how?"

"Horseback riding, she said. 'I've taken too many falls,' she said. After she'd had a few, she was talkative. You know the kind. But nice, a nice lady. A lady who just needed someone to talk to.''

TWO

THE CELLS WERE on the lower floor of the building that held the town offices and the police department. Emby had mentioned that the township's rare murder cases were usually moved to the county facility. Maria had not been judged a serious risk, but bail had been set too high for her slender resources. I was wondering about the curious omissions and generosities of her unknown benefactor when a police officer motioned for me to follow him. He led me to a bare, windowless gray-walled room with a table and several straight chairs. A moment later, another officer brought Maria Rivas into the room.

My first thought was that she was almost ridiculously young; the second, that she was extremely beautiful. The few news photos had shown dark hair, a thin upraised arm, the shielding line of a jacket, or the frozen immobility and unflattering light of a passport photo. In the flesh, Maria Rivas was a small, slight woman with splendid black hair and eyes, a fine well-shaped mouth, and the delicate aquiline nose of a Mayan princess. She stood very still and straight, with an impassive dignity at odds with her intense despairing eyes.

"How do you do," I said. "I'm Anna Peters. I run a private investigation agency and I've been hired to assist with your defense."

Her large eyes were alert and seemed comprehending, but she sat down across from me without answering.

"I met with your attorney this morning," I said. "I will go over all the material he's been given, but I wanted to meet you and also to have a look at the Skanes' house."

Her expression darkened when I mentioned the Skanes, but still she said nothing.

"What I'd like to do now is to get an account of your life at the Skanes'—how you came to work for them, how you got on with them, and what happened on the night of the fire."

There was complete silence.

"*¿Comprendes?*"

She nodded.

I was starting to feel uncomfortable. "*¿Habla ingles, señorita?*"

She nodded again.

"I can provide a translator if you'd prefer to speak Spanish."

Her face told me nothing. The middle-aged police officer who'd escorted Maria stepped over from her station at the door and said, "She doesn't speak."

"She's mute?" Emby might have mentioned that detail!

"No, they say she spoke fine before. Since the fire, she's lost the ability to speak. They didn't tell you that?"

"No, but I just came on the case today."

"They had her to the psychiatrist, even into St. Elizabeth's. Can't get a word out of her, though she understands you fine."

"I see." But of course I didn't. "Would you write answers for me?" I asked Maria Rivas.

She hesitated, then nodded, but though we started off in fine style, it was soon apparent that neither my reading knowledge of Spanish nor her written knowledge of English was going to be adequate.

"I will come back," I said. "I have a Spanish-speaking intern."

I could tell that the word was unfamiliar to her.

"A pupil, a woman learning my sort of business. She will be able to translate for me. All right?"

Maria Rivas inclined her head slightly and studied me with black, mysterious eyes.

WHEN I GOT BACK to my office, I left an acerbic message on Emby's machine, demanding the medical and psychiatric reports and asking why the hell he'd omitted any mention of our client's peculiarities. I grumbled to Martha about the waste of my time, told a delighted Rosita I needed her for a special project, then redirected my spleen toward our fraudulent developer's hidden assets. As it turned out, I had good hunting there, and I was in a much better mood when I got home with the big envelope of Skane case material in my briefcase.

Harry was in the kitchen. Since his heart attack last year, he is allowed one glass of red wine a day. He starts sipping it when he begins dinner and contrives to have it last until the end of the meal. I can usually tell what kind of day he's had by what's left in the glass when I come home. Today, the wine was already half-finished.

"How are things?"

"Lousy. Press trouble."

"Oh, that's too bad."

"Sidney came over and thinks he's got it straightened out," Harry said as he put some chicken in the frying pan. "We got those festival posters out on time, but I'm way behind now on the illustrations."

"Which are those?"

"For the Lem," Harry said.

"Oh, right. *The Futurological Congress.* That should be ideal for you." Stanislaw Lem, the Polish science fiction writer, is equally interested in the technological and the bizarre; *The Futurological Congress* was a particularly flamboyant and imaginative example of his style.

"If I can ever get on with them," Harry said, but the thought of the illustrations brightened his mood. "I'm going to try something new, an etching over aquatint, to catch the split between the comfortable world the characters think they experience and the wreckage underneath."

"I suppose the book was a sort of satire on the Communist regime in Poland."

"In part." Harry began adding garlic and chopped-up herbs to the pan. Like a lot of artists, he's a good cook, and I sat down for a minute on one of the high kitchen stools to watch him work. With his wide, rather heavy shoulders and long legs, Harry still gives an impression of size and power that is in a sharp contrast to his quick, deft movements. But though he's been good about his weight since his attack, his face is getting some lines and his hair has begun to gray. In these little signs of mortality, I see my own age reflected and realize that I'm growing old along with this man.

"That smells good. What is it?"

"Chicken Provençal. Something you like."

"I like all your cooking. Want me to fix a salad?"

"So long as you don't attempt the dressing."

"I can mix oil and vinegar as well as anyone," I said, but really I can't defend my cooking. It's not precisely dreadful, but, as my husband sometimes reminds me, it lacks conviction. Harry made a face and I washed my hands and began throwing lettuce into salad bowls. "I had a first today."

"Oh yeah?"

"A speechless client."

"Detective's delight, I should think."

"I'm not being funny. Literally without speech. She's going to have to write me answers—in Spanish, no less. And her stupid public defender let me go all the way out there and never said a word."

"Do you have to write out your questions?" Harry asked.

"No, she's not a deaf-mute. It's psychological, apparently. To do Emby justice, he may have thought it was temporary."

"It might be," my husband said. "That happened to Maya Angelou, the poet."

Harry has a fund of curious information.

"Really?"

"I read about it before she gave the poem at the inauguration. She was raped as a child, told her grandmother, and then, coincidentally, her attacker was killed. She didn't speak for years afterward."

"Well, the powers that be aren't going to wait years for Maria Rivas to regain her voice. I'm going to have to cope. It was shock, I suppose. I mean with Angelou."

"Guilt, she said. At least that's what I read."

There was food for thought, and though we spoke of other things at dinner—Harry's illustrations, a new Chinese film we wanted to see, some gossip about Jan Gorgon, his business partner—the idea returned later when I started reading through the evidence summaries and the statements from assorted Skane family members and employees.

According to the material in hand, Maria had been nurse and companion for Helena Skane for nearly two years before she began an affair with Joseph Skane. ("I'm not saying he didn't pursue her," Molly Portman, the cook had stated. "He was always after her.") Not surprisingly, this had caused strains within the Skane household. (Luisa Ceasario: "I'd hear them yelling." Question: Who? "Señora Skane and Maria.") Joseph Skane had finally come to his senses. ("God, I was ashamed. Helena meant everything to me. It was just one of those things, you know? Maria was around all the time. But I soon got over it; I told her it had to stop." Question: Told Ms. Rivas? "Yeah. Took her out to dinner. Told her it was over. Offered—*offered*, damn it—to pay her way back home. She wouldn't hear of it, couldn't accept it—though I never thought there was any danger.")

When I opened the folder with Martha's clips, Joe Skane's handsome fleshy face smiled back at me. The photo had been taken at the opening of the twentieth Beefeater's Restaurant, and Skane looked smug and prosperous, the all-conquering hero of the commercial wars. And the victim of a lover scorned? It was a formulation the press liked, if headlines like "FATAL ATTRACTION" ARSON and AN AMY FISHER WANNA-BE were any indication, and I had to admit that the evidence at hand seemed to confirm their suppositions. Both Portmans supported Luisa Ceasario's observation that relations between Mrs. Skane and Maria had deteriorated. The chauffeur, John Delano, had noticed that Joseph Skane often joined Maria in the pool for an early-morning swim. The Skane children both claimed that their parents were a happy couple, the family a happy family, before the "brief affair" with Ms. Rivas. As Emby had said, there wasn't much to work with and what there was wasn't very promising.

Nonetheless, someone was interested enough to pay my substantial rates and vulnerable enough to conceal his identity. That was one thing. Another was Maria

Rivas's extraordinary physical appearance. She struck me as the sort of woman who might produce extreme responses. It would be worth getting a fresh account of the disaster from her.

ROSITA AND I ARRIVED at the cells early the next morning. I explained the purpose of our visit to Maria again and set a pad and a pen on the table. "I want you to write your responses in Spanish, all right? Rosita will help me translate. *¿Comprendes?*"

She nodded and took the pen.

"All right. Let's start at the very beginning. When did you arrive?"

She wrote something and pushed the pad across to Rosita. "'I came in April,'" Rosita read.

"April of 1990?"

Maria wrote several lines and Rosita read them to me. "'I got my medical certificate in the fall and I worked for a time in Guatemala City. Then I signed with the agency.'"

"That's International Nursing Services?"

She nodded.

"Why did you do that? Why did you want to leave Guatemala?"

Her face was still, but her eyes darkened. For a moment, I thought she would refuse to answer. Then she wrote something hurriedly. "'Political troubles,'" Rosita translated. Maria turned the pad again. "'In April, I got a call.'"

"That was the Skanes?"

"'Right. Invalid lady needs nurse, companion. They asked if I could lift her in and out of bed and in and out of a wheelchair. I said I could, and I came as soon as I got my visa.'"

"How did the job work out?"

She looked around the room sardonically.

"I mean initially, at first. Did you get on well with Mrs. Skane?"

"'Yes. She was all right. She talked too much...and complained. Every day, she had a new complaint. But it was not hard work. I was used to hard work and fortunately she was not too heavy. I helped her up....'"

"She needed help getting out of bed?"

"'Disk trouble,'" Rosita read. "'That's what she said, but I think there was something more. Her muscles were wasting.'"

"As if she had some muscular disease?"

"'That would be my guess. She went to the doctor, but she never discussed her diagnosis. Maybe there was nothing wrong with her. She sat around in the morning and complained to me. In the afternoon, she drank. That did not leave much time for exercise.'"

"And in the evening?"

"'Bed.'"

"What time did she go to bed normally?"

"'Right after dinner—seven-thirty, eight. She had a TV. Quite often she would say to me, "Maria, just **bring up a tray.**" She liked to eat alone in her room.'"

So much for the close Skane family.

"And how did you get along with her personally?"

"'She talked, I listened. I am a good listener. I'd say, "Yes, Señora Skane, no, Señora Skane," unless she was drunk. Then she'd say, "Call me Helena" and I'd say "Yes, Helena, no, Helena." Poor Señora Skane. She was not a happy lady.'"

"When did you start looking after her grandchildren?"

Maria dug the pen angrily into the pad. "'*I am not a babysitter,*'" Rosita read. "'I explained that to her. She started to cry. I said all right, but only for a few days. For six weeks, they had me running over in the afternoon to watch those kids—though she did finally pay me extra.'"

"So your relations with Mrs. Skane were generally all right?"

She nodded.

"Right up until her death?"

Maria's glance wandered away, then she scribbled "'I didn't kill her.'"

"I didn't ask if you killed her. I asked if your relations with her had remained all right."

"'Why shouldn't they? I did my work, I understood my job.'"

"There might be other reasons. Joseph Skane says his wife grew jealous." I had Rosita repeat this in Spanish so that I could be sure Maria understood. "What about that?"

An angry scrawl ran across the paper. "'He's a lying son of a bitch.'"

"His wife wasn't jealous?"

"'No.'"

"His wife had no reason to be jealous?"

" 'No.' " Her face closed up like a safe.

"The prosecution is set to charge that you set fire to the Skane house because you wanted to eliminate Mrs. Skane. They will claim that you were jealous of her. And Joseph Skane will testify that you were having an affair with him. Translate that, too," I told Rosita.

" 'None of this is true.' "

"You didn't set the fire?"

" 'No.' "

"You weren't having an affair with Joseph Skane?"

" '*No.*' " She shook her head vigorously.

"Please tell me what happened on July fifteenth. Start with when you got up in the morning."

" 'It was a perfectly normal day. I got up at six-thirty, went for a swim, and had breakfast by seven-thirty. At eight-thirty, I awakened Señora Skane and helped her with her bath. I took up her breakfast soon after nine. Everything was fine, because the children were away.' "

"They were visiting their mother's mother, is that right?"

" 'Yes. Just that week. They promised to have a new nanny by the time the children came back. I was very pleased. I had no wish to leave the Skanes, but the children were too much on top of taking care of the señora.' "

"What else did you do that day?"

" 'I gave Señora Skane her massage and her medicine. She had various prescription drugs. Around one, I took up her lunch tray. I always sat and talked to her during lunch. Then I went downstairs to make something to eat. I made a sandwich, because I wanted to go to the shops in the mall.' "

"Where is this?"

She named the streets. " 'The crossroads stores and malls for the development.' "

"That's a fair distance, isn't it? Did you have access to a car?"

" 'It is only two or three miles. I used to walk, but then I got my *moto*.' "

"A motorcycle?"

"More like a scooter," Rosita said. *"Motocicleta pequeña, sí?"*

Maria nodded.

"Where did you go?"

" 'I went around Penney's and then the Green Tree Shop. Then I went to the gas station and filled up my *moto* and the can.' "

"Why the can? Ask her what her mileage is on the *moto*," I told Rosita.

" 'Seventy-five to eighty miles per gallon.' "

"Ask her where she was going. With an extra gallon and a half, she'd have enough for a considerable distance."

Rosita repeated the question in Spanish, and Maria's expression suddenly became opaque. She hesitated a moment, then wrote rapidly.

"She says she likes to have extra so she doesn't have to go down to the gas station so often," Rosita explained.

"So you'd bought gas there before?"

Maria nodded.

"When did you leave the center?" Rosita repeated this in Spanish so that Maria understood I wanted the time.

"'Around four-thirty.'"

"And when you got back, what did you do with the can of gas?"

She shook her head and scrawled. "'I put it in the garage at the back beside where I park my *moto.*'"

"Was that the usual place?"

Rosita said, "She says she always kept it there."

"Who would have known that?"

"'Anyone who was in the garage.'"

"Were the Skanes ever in the garage, or just their chauffeur?"

"'All of them. Usually they called John to bring round the cars, but sometimes they got their own.'"

"Did you have anything more to do with the can of gas?"

"'I never saw the can again.'"

"And what did you do once you got back in the house?"

"'I changed my clothes and checked with Molly....'"

"Molly Portman, the cook?"

"'Yes, to see when the señora would eat. I took up the señora's dinner around seven. I brought her tray down half an hour later. The others were all gone by that time. I ate my dinner and washed the dishes. Then I went up to my room.'"

"What time would that be?"

"'Nearly nine. I put on the TV.'"

"What did you watch?"

She shrugged her shoulders and scrawled a few lines.
"'I don't remember. Maybe the mysterious show,'"
Rosita translated.

I looked at Rosita.

"Unsolved Mysteries?" she suggested, and Maria
nodded.

"'I did some sewing. The señora was always losing
buttons and tearing hems. I ironed a couple shirts.
There was a movie on TV. I start to watch that. Then I
fell asleep.'"

"You were watching TV in bed?"

"'No. I finished the ironing. I sat down on the bed
and then—I don't know... I must have fallen asleep.'"

She was still for a moment as if thoughtful.

"When did you wake up?" I asked.

Maria's face changed. She had laid the pen down and
for a moment she hesitated to pick it up. When she
started to write, even her script looked different, jagged and nervous. "'When I smelled smoke.'"

"Did you hear the alarm? I believe they had smoke
detectors."

She shook her head. "'All I remember is the smell
of smoke. Very strong in the dark. I thought maybe I'd
left the iron on,'" Rosita read.

"Wait a minute," I said. "You said you fell asleep
watching the TV. Had you turned the lights off? The
TV?"

She shook her head vigorously, obviously agitated.
"'No, I remember that the light by my bed was on, the

TV was playing, and the light by my door was on, too.' "

"You're sure about that?"

" 'Yes, yes.' "

"What did you do when you smelled the smoke?"

" 'I got up right away. I tried the light by my bed first, but there was nothing. I thought it was the ironing board, that I'd left the iron on and caused a fire. I was afraid I'd get burned while trying to find the ironing board to shut off the iron.' "

"You didn't call for help?"

" 'I didn't think it was anything serious. I had in my mind that it was the iron burning the pad, but the iron was off. The power was all off. It was totally dark.' "

I could see her shivering. If she had set the fire, it had certainly scared the hell out of her.

" 'I started to cough. I thought, I'll get to the window, but I forgot that all the windows were sealed. The smoke was getting worse. When I pulled open the curtain, I saw a red glow and flames in the center of the house.' "

"That's looking toward Mrs. Skane's room?"

" 'Yes. I ran across the room, looking for the door. I couldn't find it. Then I fell into the ironing board and realized I'd gotten turned around. Now it was smoky, really smoky, and when I opened the door, the hall was hot, very hot. I started toward the main stair, calling to warn Señora Skane. I was calling, calling, but there was no reply, no sound. Then I saw the flames in the atrium.' "

"The atrium was visible from the corridor? There wasn't a door or anything?"

"'Everything was open. The flames were rising right to the roof. The little trees, the caged finches, everything was burning. I started to run and then the fire was in the corridor and I couldn't go any farther.'"

She lifted both her hands suddenly and gestured as Rosita translated.

"The fire exploded?"

She nodded, her hands still raised, and tears filled her eyes. I asked the guard whether she could bring Maria something to drink. The guard returned a moment later with a Styrofoam cup of water. Maria took a sip and regained control of herself.

"What did you do then?"

"'I ran back past my room and down the far stair.'"

"That would be the stair at the east corner of the house?"

She nodded.

"'By that time, I could hear the fire engines. I got out the door. John was standing on the lawn.'"

"John Delano, the chauffeur?"

"'Yes. He had a flashlight.'"

"There still were no lights anywhere about the house or grounds?"

She thought for a moment. "'None in the house. The other houses and the drive were lighted. John was shouting, "Is everyone out? Is Mrs. Skane out?" I tried to tell him that I thought the señora was still inside. Then the firemen arrived. They tried to get through the windows, but by that time it was too late.'"

Maria put down the pen, folded both arms across her chest as if she was freezing cold, and closed her eyes.

ON THE WAY BACK to the office, I asked Rosita what she thought of Maria's statement and whether she thought our client was telling the truth.

"I think she was telling the truth about the fire," Rosita said carefully.

"She certainly seemed upset."

"About the rest, I am not so sure."

Neither was I. The whole business of buying the gas bothered me, and I had the unpleasant feeling that Maria was lying about her reasons.

"But surely the fire is the important thing," Rosita said.

"Indeed. But arson cases can be awfully difficult to prove." Or, for that matter, to defend. Either Ms. Rivas was going to have to come up with a much better story or we were going to have to know a great deal more about life in the Skane family compound.

THREE

I CAUGHT UP with Joseph Skane in a solid old building that had been renovated and refurbished with the help of one of the more notorious HUD grants. Poverty among the coterie of politicos, developers, and community brokers concerned had been forestalled unto at least their third generation, and a bevy of the well-connected had come to roost amid marble foyers, luxuriant plants, walnut paneling, and designer lights. Skane's firm had a big suite on the third floor of this corporate Taj Mahal; a gold-leaf sign in front announced Skane Corporation, Skane Enterprises, and Beefeaters, Incorporated. The interior was equally lavish. Skane Corporation ran to rain forest-depleting panels of rosewood and other exotics, thick pale rugs, massive desks, and leather seating. Scattered around the offices was a nice little collection of seventeenth-century drawings, a tiny Canaletto, and a fine group of minor Impressionists.

I had plenty of time to appreciate all this splendor because the leader of the Skane domain was in no hurry to see me. I had time to look at the pictures, to flip through the collection of glossy shelter magazines, and to notice the extraordinary number of attractive young women with important hair, perfect nails, and diminutive skirts who flittered from one office to the next. At last, one of these clerical goddesses came over and announced that Mr. Skane could spare me a minute.

We went down a short corridor and into what appeared to be a cube of mirrored glass, an ultramodern touch totally at odds with the fine old nineteenth-century structure. Inside was a luxurious executive suite with overstuffed leather chairs and some of Leroy Neiman's more vulgar sports paintings. The glass proved to be one-way. Skane was sitting comfortably behind his desk, smoking a cigar and watching the progress of a leggy young woman delivering copy to the various work stations beyond.

"This is Anna Peters," my guide said.

"Come in; come in. Good to meet you. You're with…" He turned to the secretary. "Who's she with, honey?"

"Executive Security," I said.

"Insurance, we've got," he said with a laugh. "My premiums are so high, I'd make money if the whole pile went up."

"Executive Security is an investigation and security agency," I said. "I've been asked to make some inquiries for Maria Rivas's defense counsel."

"Yeah, yeah. Just a joke. Lighten up, I tell my staff. I'll call you when I need you, honey," he told the secretary, and she pranced away in her too-high heels.

"Gorgeous girl," he said to no one in particular. His eyes followed her out through the office beyond.

What a cretin, I thought.

"Maria Rivas is a beautiful woman," I remarked.

Joseph Skane dropped his feet off the desk and slumped heavily in his chair. "Maria is a psychopath," he said. "Listen, we did everything for her, right? Nice room, super house, swimming pools indoors and out, bowling lanes, tennis, squash. A car—we taught her how to drive, you know. Is she content?"

"I was curious how you came to hire her." I'd decided it would be safest to begin on a neutral topic.

"The wife needed care." He sniffed ostentatiously and wiped his nose. "I used to—God forgive me—I used to think Helena exaggerated her complaints. You know, women get to a certain age and they're not the same; they begin to let things bother them."

"I wouldn't know," I said. I guessed I had a few years on both him and the late Helena.

"A little disk trouble, a little emotional upset, we thought. Jesus, comes the fire, she couldn't even make it downstairs!" He wiped his eyes. "And the thing is, who knew the worst of her condition? Who knew?"

"Her family?" I guessed innocently.

"Maria Rivas. She was the trained nurse, or so we'd been led to expect."

"By International Nursing Services."

"That's right. We're suing them," he said. "My lawyers have good hopes."

"I'm puzzled why you dealt with a foreign nurse in the first place. Surely the D.C. area has nursing services, trained LPNs and RNs?"

"You know what those bastards charge? Shit, if I'd wanted to really clean up, I'd have gone into nursing services. Not"—he gestured to me—"that I'd have denied Helena anything, God bless her. But she couldn't stand waste. We had a nurse for a week, and she said to me, she said, 'Joseph, I can't see a hundred-plus a day.' That's what she said. She said she'd rather have a little something extra for herself. I mean, what did she need a nurse for? Bring her medicine, rub her back, keep her company. You don't need a Ph.D. to do that, you know."

"So you got Maria. What was her salary?"

"Three hundred a week, plus room and board." He held up his hands. "Hey, I even paid Social Security tax. I like to do things right. And what did it get us?" He shook his head. "Poor Helena," he said.

"You understand that I have been employed to assist in Maria Rivas's defense. I interpret that as doing my best to find out what happened. That's my job."

"Honey, you're going to be disappointed. No doubt she did it. Shit, I've been kicking myself ever since. I've been saying, Joe, how could you be so dumb? Not to see it coming. Not to have foreseen."

"You have no doubts that Maria set the fire?"

"She bought the gas. She brought it home. She was the only one in the house that night, and she and John were the only ones in the compound. Listen, I agreed to see you because, what the heck, you've got to earn a living, too. This is your job, right? So I'm doing you a favor to keep you from going out on a limb. Just remember, you can't trust anything Maria says."

"Maria isn't *saying* anything now."

For the first time, he looked at me with real concentration. "Still?"

I nodded. "She is providing a written statement."

"Of course it's a shame, a damn shame. Hell, I'm willing to take some of the blame. Don't think I don't feel bad about screwing around with her, but I lost Helena to that psychopath."

"Just how did it happen?" I asked.

"You know how it is. A pretty girl is around all the time. You go out for a drink. . . ."

"Maria seems to have been on call most of the day," I observed.

"In a manner of speaking, I meant. I'd see her at the pool; we'd stop by the wet bar. The pool cabana has a complete wet bar. Great for parties. Kinda detail not everyone thinks of in a home. See, that's the touch in our developments—and in Beefeaters, too: Put in everything no matter what it costs—PIENMWIC!"

"Your house certainly has that look," I said.

"Well, it was only natural, wasn't it, that Maria might get the wrong idea?" He turned as he spoke to watch another of the Skane Corporation's striking office staff.

"Maria denies any personal involvement with you. Why do you think that is?"

"These Latin girls—good Catholics, most of them. They're funny about sex. They want it, but they don't want to admit it."

"Surely there's another reason," I said. "No affair, no motive."

"Trust me," Skane said with the confidence of a man who thinks himself irresistible.

"Neither you nor your wife had any other enemies?"

"Listen, Helena was the sweetest woman in the world."

"That doesn't quite answer the question," I said.

"All right, all right. Everyone who makes as much money as I have makes enemies. You may not know that. But that's business enemies. This is personal. This is my family, for God's sake." He leaned over his desk, his gabby bonhomie gone. "I'm going to nail that bitch's ass to the wall. You tell her that and see she understands it."

THAT AFTERNOON I headed back to the Skanes' suburban turf. On the way, I stopped at the gas station where Maria had purchased the can of gas and confirmed that she stopped there regularly, almost always filling up her auxiliary can at the same time. That was reassuring but hardly significant, and I went on to the Skanes'. The main building was still boarded up and apparently untouched. Presumably, they were waiting for the insurance reports, but it seemed odd that Skane was not more anxious to begin repairs. I wondered who his insurance carrier was and how much the main Skane house was worth.

In the meantime, I introduced myself to the security guard on duty, then walked back to the garage. I'd hoped to find Luisa and Antonia Ceasario about, but the door that led to the apartments upstairs was locked. The only sign of life was one of the open garage doors.

Inside, a thin man in dark pants and a black T-shirt was polishing a big white Mercedes with a piece of chamois. He had a pale, angular face and his eyes were hidden behind very dark sunglasses.

"What can I do for you?" he asked.

I introduced myself and handed him one of my cards.

"John Delano. I've already spoken to the police," he said.

"I'm sure they were very thorough, but it's sometimes useful to see things for oneself. I'd hoped to speak to you and to the inside staff, the Portmans and the Ceasario sisters."

"They're gone," he said.

"For the day, you mean?"

"Naw. Gone, as in fired. Not that it makes any difference now. Mr. Skane, he's moved out. The kids are on their own. The house is closed up."

"I see. Would you know where they went?"

"Don't know about the Ceasarios. The Portmans were talking retirement, last I heard. Somewhere in Florida."

"But you don't have an address?"

"Lady, all I know is that I come downstairs one day and a cab's waiting for Luisa and Antonia and the Portmans are loading up a U-Haul trailer."

"When was this?"

"Right after the fire. Excuse me; I've gotta wipe these windows."

"A beautiful car," I said.

"Very nice. Handles well, too."

"You were here the night of the fire, weren't you?"

"Yeah. I thought I'd be gone, too."

"Oh, why was that?"

"The boss seemed set to make a clean sweep. But there wasn't much he could say to me: My rooms are on the back. I didn't hear anything and I didn't notice anything. You know how it is with the stereo on, and we never lost power."

"But the main house did?"

"Sure. The fire musta got to the circuit box or something shorted it out right away."

"How did you notice it?"

"I got up to get a beer. I'd been in the pit—sorry, on the computer net, with a group of old biplane fanciers. Anyway, I get up; I hear a funny noise. When I look out the back, I see this red glow in the pond. I call nine-one-one and run across to see what I can do."

"This would have been close to ten?"

"Yeah. I couldn't get near the back—the fire was already bad. I go around to the front and almost run into Maria tearing out the side door."

"What did she tell you?"

"Nothing. That was the weird thing. She looked as if she was screaming, but no sound was coming out. I asked her where the Mrs. was. She pointed upstairs. But by then, there wasn't anything I could do."

"What sort of person is Maria?"

He worked with the chamois for a minute, then said, "Nice."

I waited.

"Very quiet, you know. Though her English was pretty good and would have gotten better if she hadn't spent most of her free time with Luisa and Antonia."

There was something in his voice, and I had the feeling he would rather she'd spent time with him. He worked away with the chamois. "'Course you never know, do you? If you just see people at work."

"What about her relations with Joseph Skane?"

"What about them?"

"He claims they had an affair."

John Delano shrugged and there was another long pause, as if this were a painful topic. "I wouldn't know," he said in a neutral voice. "I'm hired to take care of the vehicles."

"Did you ever see them together?"

"They both liked to swim. Sometimes they were in the pool at the same time."

"Anything unusual about that?"

"Naw. The boss, he likes pretty women—and company. Some guys, you know, are kinda standoffish. Don't want to see the help. It's like you're supposed to be invisible. Mr. Skane, now, he likes a crowd around him. He'd say, 'Come on, have a swim. Take a beer.' That's if he was in a good mood. In a bad mood, he'd take your head off. You have to know how to deal with him."

"You've been with him how long?"

"Nearly five years. We get along all right."

"Ever drive him and Maria anywhere?"

The chamois swept smoothly over the car's pearly white surface. "Just once. A big serious occasion. He took her out to dinner."

"One of his own restaurants?"

"No way. Little place I'd never heard of over in Annapolis. Very quiet. Ultraexpensive."

"But just that one time?"

"Far as I know."

That certainly confirmed one thing Joe Skane had said. "This was recently?" I asked.

"Naw. Couple years ago, I guess."

"Really?" Skane's account had definitely implied his offer to buy off Maria had been a recent thing—just before the fire. "And do you know what the evening was about?"

"I just drive the car."

"You said a 'big serious occasion.'"

"Like some big business deal. Same atmosphere. You know, as if something was going to get settled."

"And did it?"

John Delano shrugged. "He came out looking mad as hell. I think she'd been crying. Beats me. They didn't neither one of them say a word all the way home."

FOUR

SABRINA AND ARNOLD BACH lived to the left of the garage, a good hundred yards away from the main house but still in the shadow, so to speak, of that monumental building. Not that the Bachs were living like poor relations; they owned their own massive neo-Georgian house with a hipped roof and big arched Palladian windows. The drive that curled around by their front door had solid granite curbings and marked off immaculate ovals of lawn and shrubbery.

I used one of the massive lion's head knockers on the oak double doors and heard a chime ring inside the house.

"I'll get it, Nancy," someone said, and the door opened. A young blond woman in a black velour warm-up suit stood in the doorway. She was in her stocking feet, holding an elaborate pair of tennis shoes and wearing an equally elaborate diamond tennis bracelet. A racket as big as a butterfly net rested against the wall, amid ball cans and an oversized gym bag.

"Oh?" She had clearly been expecting someone else.

"Mrs. Bach?"

"That's right."

I handed over my card. "I have been asked to assist in Maria Rivas's defense. I know it must be painful to discuss anything about the fire, but I would appreciate a few minutes of your time.''

She had a small well-proportioned face, brown eyes, and a tense, rather nervous expression. The nails on her otherwise-beautifully tended hands were bitten to the quick.

''I can't imagine why I'd want to do anything to help Maria,'' she said.

''I understand your feelings,'' I said, ''but Maria has not even gone on trial yet. No one knows whether or not she set the fire, and there isn't much more than circumstantial evidence.'' That was stretching things a little but not too much. ''I'm sure you want to know who really killed your mother.''

''I don't have any doubts at all,'' she said, but she stepped back so that I could enter.

''You look as if you're on your way to a tennis match.''

''My lesson. I thought you were my doubles partner.''

''I play a very poor game of tennis.''

''So few people get good coaching,'' she said complacently. I sensed that Sabrina Bach did not wear her wealth lightly.

''I just wanted to ask about your mother's relationship with Maria. Maria had taken care for her for—what, almost two years?''

''That's right. She seemed to be very competent.''

''So your mother was satisfied with her care?''

Mrs. Bach gave a sigh of exasperation. "Mother wanted to get rid of Maria. That was one reason she sent her over to fill in when Naomi left us suddenly."

"Surely she wouldn't have kept Maria for two years if she wasn't satisfied."

"It was just lately. I guess Joseph's told you about his... his little fling with Maria?"

"Why didn't your mother fire her?"

"That's what I'd have done. But Mother hated unpleasantness. She hated upsets. She thought it would be better just to ease Maria out. That was Mother's approach to everything." Her daughter was clearly made of different stuff.

"I understand they quarrelled—Maria and your mother, I mean."

"Who told you that?"

"It's in the police statements. A number of the staff mentioned raised voices, arguments."

"Mother had come to depend on Maria. She felt betrayed. But if you have the police statements, you'll know what I told them: Mother found out that Joseph had his eye on Maria and she made a fuss."

"Yet no one felt uneasy about leaving your mother alone with Maria the night of the fund-raiser?"

"We never imagined," Sabrina said hastily. "We thought it was over. Joe had spoken to Maria; Mother told me so. It was over, or so she said."

"Or so she believed?"

"Mother was good about believing what she wanted to believe," Sabrina admitted. "She's—she was not the way she used to be. I mean after her illness. She used to be outgoing, charming, wonderful company. After she took sick, she wasn't the same person. All she wanted to do was to sit in her room with the television on. She never went in the pool or to the club or to the theater. She hardly even went to the greenhouse anymore.''

''And this illness was why Maria was hired in the first place?''

''Yes. But having Maria enabled my mother to go into a shell. She just never came out.''

''You mentioned the club. That's a golf club?''

''Long Hills. Not the dinky little club in this development. Very exclusive. Very nice, really. Mother hated golf. She went to play bridge.''

''Did she play with anyone regularly?''

''Elizabeth Sisko and Evelyn Demey were the card sharks. I don't know who else. Mother went twice a week, Tuesday and Thursday afternoons, for as long as I can remember. That's before she got sick. After that, she rarely played.''

We heard the sound of a car on the drive.

''And your mother's illness?'' I asked quickly. ''What was her diagnosis exactly?''

''That'll be my doubles partner. You'll have to leave now.'' Sabrina opened the door, waved, and called, ''I'll be right out, Claire.''

''Thank you for your time,'' I said.

''Don't bother trying to see my brother,'' Sabrina said as she shoved her feet into her sneakers. ''Tony's not home. This whole thing has hit him very hard.'' She scooped up her gear, including a chic black warm-up jacket. She really did look very nice in athletic mourning. Sabrina closed the door behind us and hurried over to her friend's BMW. I walked toward where I'd parked, then changed my mind. The sporty old Thunderbird convertible parked in front of Tony Skane's house didn't look as if it belonged to the help. I crossed the big circular drive and rang his bell.

A thin-faced Asian man opened the door and studied my card for a moment before asking me into a black marble-floored foyer as big as our living room. The walls had a thick charcoal gray covering of some sort and a lot of white leather chairs were grouped beside ornate brass and marble tables along the walls. Except for an extraordinarily detailed painting of Wrigley Field, the room had the respectful air of having just left the decorator's hands.

"...thought I'd measure."

"A goddamn waste of your time," a masculine voice answered. "I like the room just as it is."

"If I'm to be living here..." the woman's voice responded.

"I don't know how many times I have to tell you—it's not going to work."

"...just upset...need support at a time like this."

"I need for you to get the hell out of my life."

Something fell on the floor with a crash. A door toward the rear of the foyer opened and a tall, rather plump woman with a great deal of reddish blond hair rushed out. She cleared off two of the little tables as she swept past me and ran outside to the sports car. There was a roar, the ominous sound of overstressed gears, then the squeal and spatter of tires on gravel.

A moment later, Tony Skane appeared, dressed in a T-shirt and jeans. He was small like his sister, with the same neat features and slight build, but with brown hair and light eyes. He sniffled as if he had a cold and said, "Some people won't take no for an answer."

"Your friend in the sports car?"

"Would-be fiancée in *my* sports car. She'll have the gearing ruined. It's the house," he added. "Sue's crazy about the house. 'Course, she should be. She and Mother did the design. Do you like it?"

"Chilly but impressive," I said.

"It's like a corporate boardroom," he said. "Wonderful if you're going to be doing company parties."

"Maybe a few too many breakables."

"Hector buys cheap things for the foyer. Hector," he called. "Hector, bring the brush and shovel." Then he opened the door to the living room. "So, you're..." He made a production of pulling out my card and taking a look at it. "Anna Peters. Insurance?"

"Investigation."

There was a flicker of intelligence in his eyes, as if his dithery charm had been a little comic turn. "Sit down and be comfortable. Are you part of the fire investigation?"

"No. I'd imagine your insurance carrier is handling that."

"Yes, I guess so. Old State Assurance, I think it is. Yes, they've been sifting the rubble."

"And doubtless checking the policy."

"The policies," he said. "I'm afraid they're set to take quite a hit on this one."

"I should think." What I couldn't think was why he was telling me this unsolicited.

"But you are . . ."

"Interested in Maria Rivas. My firm has been hired to assist in her defense."

He sat back in his chair and began fiddling with the thick pleats that ornamented the arms. "I'm surprised you had the nerve to come see us," he said.

"Who else am I going to talk to? Maria Rivas lived in your house for over two years."

"I don't see what there is to talk about. Who else could have done it?"

"Any number of people. Your father may have business enemies. His companies employ a lot of people. One of them could be disgruntled. This must have been a massive construction job. Maybe someone didn't get paid what he thought he should have. Perhaps there were disputes in the family. I don't know. I don't see that Maria had a particularly good motive."

"She quarreled with my mother," he said. Tony Skane got up as he spoke. He walked over to the modern marble fireplace, lifted a box from the mantel, and took out a cigarette.

"Do you know what they argued about?"

Tony Skane took time to light his cigarette and to watch the column of smoke reflected in the big mirror over the mantel. "Mother thought Dad was paying too much attention to Maria."

"And was he?"

"He says so."

"What do you think?"

Tony Skane raised one eyebrow. "I can't think why he'd lie and upset Mother."

I could think of some reasons but kept my mouth shut.

"Have you talked to Sabrina?" he asked.

"I just came from her house. She was on her way to play tennis."

"Did she tell you I was out?"

"Yes, as a matter of fact."

He nodded at this and returned to his chair. "She's fond of playing the protective big sister."

"Do you need protection?"

He drew reflectively on his cigarette. "Let's just say that's a matter of dispute."

"I think you're pretty safe today," I said. "I want to know who knew Maria well."

"I wouldn't know," he said so airily, I was immediately suspicious. "*I* hardly knew her."

"What about John Delano? I got the feeling he found her attractive."

Tony Skane frowned. "He had almost no contact with her. He's not on the place all that much."

"There are other places to meet," I observed. I was thinking about Maria's *moto* and her regular trips to the gas station. "She had a motorbike and bought gas for it regularly. Any idea where she went?"

"No, but she definitely wasn't meeting John," he said quickly. "The only people she was close to were the Ceasarios. They worked for Mother."

"I understand they've both gone. Is that right?"

"Naturally. Now that the house is closed, there was no work for them."

"Would you know where they went?"

He shrugged.

"There will be tax documents to send them, won't there? Where will their W-two forms be sent? Surely there would be a forwarding address."

"They weren't very sophisticated people."

"What about the Portmans?"

"They didn't know Maria well. I don't think they got along."

"No?"

"The Portmans are English. Dad liked their accents. Thought they added class. Very professional, a bit stodgy. They didn't like working with 'foreigners.'"

"And where did they go?"

"Somewhere in Florida."

I waited.

"Somewhere in the Sarasota area."

"They'd been with your parents a long time, hadn't they?"

"Yes, and they worked for Mother's family before she married my dad."

That was interesting. I'd assumed that the money in the family had all been Joseph Skane's doing.

"Mother was used to trained help. I mean well-trained professional people. Dad wanted to hire whoever was cheapest. It drove Mother crazy."

"You have a professional cleaning firm."

"Yes, and the lawn service, too. I'm used to it," he said philosophically. "Mother said it was like living in a motel."

"Maria was well trained?"

"She was just waiting to pass the language exam for her nursing license."

"Would she have managed that?"

"Sooner or later."

"Was she in love with your father?"

"No," he said. "No, she wasn't. She didn't particularly like him." He seemed very positive, considering his claim that he scarcely knew her.

"She used to go swimming with him."

"That's not quite right. He used to go swimming whenever he saw her in the pool."

"She objected to that?"

"I got that impression," he said. "Of course, it was just an impression."

I wondered about that. "Why didn't Maria leave, then?" I asked. "She was a trained nurse. There are plenty of people needing nursing care."

"I suppose she got to like the life."

"Or someone else around the place?"

"Really, I never got involved in her personal life. It was none of our business. Patriarchy is finished, I'm told." He fiddled with his cigarette and tapped the ash off carefully, then stood up. "I don't think I can tell you anything more."

"Thank you for your time. If you find the Ceasarios' address, perhaps you could call me?"

"It's very unlikely, but I'll keep your card."

I had reached the door when he said, "How is Maria doing? I assume you've talked to her."

"Talked at her," I said. "She isn't speaking."

He turned away toward the fireplace, but I could see the tight line of his jaw in the mirror. "I assume that will pass. Won't it?" he asked with a touch of anxiety.

"No one seems to know. I suspect being in prison is bad for her."

"Perhaps you'll get her off," he said.

"I wouldn't count on it," I replied and saw myself out.

I'd been hoping to run into the insurance investigators, but the Skane compound was all quiet. I decided that the only other possibility was the gardener, who, if I remembered Emby correctly, was also longtime staff. I walked behind the garage and through some shrubbery toward an ornate glasshouse. There was a row of cold frames to one side and a stout white-haired man was kneeling by the closest of them, working on some plants. He looked up when he heard my feet on the path.

"Afternoon," he said.

"I was admiring the greenhouse."

"That's a copy of an English Victorian glasshouse."

"Beautiful. Is it as efficient as the newer models?"

"All the latest material and the best glass—computer-controlled louvers, solar heat, everything your heart could desire." His broad, handsome face looked about sixty, but his hands suggested he was well into his seventies, an idea strengthened by the stiff and painful way he got to his feet. "I don't mind being down," he said, "and I don't mind being up. It's the getting one place or the other that's hard."

"An occupational hazard?"

"You might have something there. I've been in greenhouses getting on for sixty years. Touch of rheumatism. Now, it could be the damp. Yes, it could."

"This looks like a big operation."

He laughed. "This is an amusement. I'm only part-time, something to keep me out of trouble." He smiled again and asked, "And who might you be, if you don't mind my asking?"

I introduced myself and handed him a card.

He took a look at it and said, "I'm Andrew Malpas. I'm not needing a detective, I'm sure."

"I've been asked to assist Maria Rivas's defense counsel."

"A shame," he said. "She's a nice little lass, not the kind you'd think would do such a thing."

"Did you see much of her?"

"She came up every day to get the flowers. She was very fond of the tender tropicals. Said they reminded her of home. I started some bougainvillea for her this last winter."

"The flowers were for the house?"

"Oh, yes, Mrs. Skane wanted fresh flowers every day. Mr. Skane, he'd just have ordered them, but she liked the idea of growing them right on the place. She liked to have a small display at the flower shows and to donate plants to the museum."

"Which you grew for her."

"Oh yes. But under her direction, of course," he said, and winked. "Ladies like Mrs. Skane enjoy getting the credit."

"So I can imagine. Was she easy to work for?"

"She was very fair and businesslike. She was used to employing help and treated them right. Not like Mr. Skane. He has only one question: 'What will it cost?'"

I looked around the grounds in surprise. "He certainly seems to have opened his wallet on occasion," I said.

"I'm not saying he didn't spend money. What I'm saying is, he wanted to do everything on the cheap—cut-rate. Do you want to know what the best building is on this place?"

I nodded.

"Right there behind you, that glasshouse. Top quality, every inch of it. That was Mrs. Skane's doing. He would have cut corners on every detail. It might have looked the same, but it wouldn't have lasted like that one will—not that they'll know the difference."

"Aren't they going to keep it running?"

"They don't care about flowers. But I'm here till they tell me otherwise, and while I'm here, I keep busy."

He started to begin his slow descent into a working position and I said, "Could I take a look in the greenhouse?"

"Suit yourself. Not much in it now." He opened the door and motioned for me to step inside. "Worth seeing in the winter, though."

The house had a rather high and awkward sill. "Not very convenient for a woman in a wheelchair."

"You mean Mrs. Skane?"

"Yes. She was quite handicapped, wasn't she?"

"She had bad days. Then she used the chair. On good days, she walked with a cane."

"But Maria Rivas was hired as a full-time nurse."

"Who hired her?" The gardener asked. "That's what I always wanted to know. It wasn't Mrs. Skane's idea. I know that for a fact, because she stood right where you're standing and told me so. 'Course, she was a little under the weather at the time, if you know what I mean. She said, 'They're watching me. They think I don't know it, but they're wrong.' She wasn't happy about a nurse coming at all."

"And later? How did they get on?"

"I never saw them together. Neither one was a gossip, if that's any help."

For all I knew, it might be. I thanked the gardener for his time and went back to fetch my car. The chauffeur was out front, closing up the garage, and I think he was surprised that I was still around.

"You've had the grand tour," he remarked.

"Best to see people as soon as you can," I said. "By the way, is Maria Rivas's motor scooter still around?"

He threw up the overhead door and pointed toward the back of the garage, behind the Mercedes, a Volvo, and two station wagons was a sizable bike rack, holding three impressive ten-speed racing models, a mountain bike, an assortment of children's models, and the motor scooter.

"Was this where she usually kept the gas can?"

"Right. She always liked to have a little extra."

"Did she take long trips somewhere?"

"She was off Mondays," Delano said. "Mondays, she was usually away all day."

"Do you know where she went?"

"She never said."

"Did she have friends in the area? Relatives?"

He shrugged. "No idea."

I went over and checked the odometer. "Do you have any idea how long she'd had the machine?"

"About a year," Delano said. "Bought it new down at the cycle shop."

"New?" I said. That was interesting. In roughly a year of Mondays, Maria had put nearly thirty thousand miles on the machine.

FIVE

THE LONG HILLS Cricket Club looked as venerable as its name suggested. The main building was a sprawling old wood-frame structure with a wide veranda surrounded by hollies and boxwood hedges. Behind it, presumably on what had once been the cricket ground, were well-appointed pools, tennis courts, and changing houses. A very green, heavily treed golf course ran all around, and from the comfortable wicker chairs on the veranda, the club members could watch the progress of the players before adjourning to the air-conditioned precincts of the clubhouse proper for the bar, the social rooms, or the bridge tables. It was Thursday afternoon, the card sharks were expected, and the club steward was trying with admirable patience to convince me that players of the seriousness of Elizabeth Sisko and Evelyn Demey could not be disturbed.

"I understand they never start before two p.m.," I said. "Sabrina Bach was really very insistent that I speak to them."

"I'm afraid there's nothing," he began when a tanned white-haired woman in an elegant camel-colored pantsuit stalked into the hall. She had a resonant bourbon-cured voice. "Henry, any sign of that damn Jane Paget yet?"

"I'm sorry, Mrs. Demey, no sign of her. I did try calling the house, but she's probably on her way."

"We haven't had a good game since Helena Skane took sick. If there's one thing I can't stand, it's unserious, unpunctual, unreliable cardplayers."

"Perhaps an unavoidable delay," the steward murmured.

"If you played cards, Henry, you'd know there are no unavoidable delays. She can find herself another game. Can't bid worth a damn, anyway. Do you play bridge?" she asked me.

"I used to play quite a lot."

"Splendid. Henry, sign in Ms. . . . ?"

"Peters," I said, "Anna Peters. Actually, I came here hoping to see you and Liz Sisko."

"Really?" Mrs. Demey headed through a pair of double doors to a big sunny room with comfortable-looking chairs, a marble fireplace, rows of club photos, and fading chintz curtains. Several card tables were set out in the center of the room. "Liz's at the table. We thought we'd get started with a hand, but Jane's late as usual. We're not supposed to know you, are we?"

"No," I said. "I'm a private investigator. I've been asked to make some inquiries into Mrs. Skane's death for Maria Rivas's defense counsel."

"Well," she said, "that'll at least make a change from the usual club gossip. Listen up, gals, we've found our fourth and she's going to get us to talk scandal. Anna Peters, Liz Sisko and Patsy O'Connnor. You're playing with me, so I hope to God you bid better than Jane does.''

"Cut for the deal?" Patsy asked. She was a chubby sandy-haired woman in her mid-forties, with a nice line in diamond rings. She opened a fresh pack of cards. Liz, slim, dark—a bit younger than the others—drew the high card, reshuffled, and dealt. I was cheered to see a pair of kings.

"One spade," Liz said. "You're new to the area?"

"I'm investigating Helena Skane's death."

"Two spades," offered Evelyn. "For the defense counsel."

"I pass," said Patsy. "You're trying to get that nurse off?"

"If I find she didn't do it."

"*Someone* obviously set the fire," Liz said.

"Two clubs," I said. "It didn't have to be Maria Rivas."

"I pass," said Liz. "I heard she had her reasons."

Evelyn gave a husky laugh. "With those reasons, half the women in town are suspect." She saw my look. "Joe Skane was notorious. Though how much went beyond the pinch-and-tickle stage is a matter of dispute." She returned to her hand and bid two hearts.

"You all knew Helena Skane well?" I asked.

"Dear, we'd played twice a week forever."

"You could say," Patsy said, "that we knew the story of her life."

"That's the story I'm interested in."

"Gossip," said Evelyn, "but don't neglect the cards."

"Sorry," Patsy said. "I pass."

I considered the points in my hand and decided there was no point in being too conservative. "Three hearts," I said.

Evelyn raised an eyebrow but said nothing.

"Did the Skanes have a happy marriage?" I asked.

"No," said Patsy.

"I don't know," Evelyn said. "What's happiness? At least Joe Skane isn't boring."

"They got on all right," Liz said, "considering."

"She had her own life," Patsy said. "She knew how to occupy herself. She was never waiting around for Joe to do anything."

"Of course, she had a really sharp mind."

"And she'd had the best of educations."

"I better pass," Liz said.

"Her family had money?" I asked.

"Soup and frozen foods," said Patsy. Evelyn passed.

"I'd gotten the impression from the news stories that the fortune was all Joe Skane's doing."

"That's the impression you're supposed to get," Patsy said. "He's got an ego as big as the Ritz. But she gave him his start. Her money bought the first Beefeaters, didn't it?"

"Dears, we heard every detail of the deal right here," Evelyn said. "You bidding or you passing, Patsy?"

"I pass. And the business would still be as sound as Fort Knox if she'd stayed in charge."

I passed and played the opening lead, a conservative six of clubs that seemed to please my partner.

"Would the firm have grown the way it has without him?" I asked.

"How it's grown is what I wonder," Liz said. "I'll give Helena a lot of credit, though. She drew the line at risking her own money."

"She said a thousand times, 'Family money is for the children,' didn't she?" Patsy asked.

"Was she reluctant to keep investing in the firm?"

"So it seems. She told me she'd been under pressure the last few years," Evelyn said. "She told me that herself."

"Pressure?" I asked. "You mean to put more money in Beefeaters?"

"Sure," Evelyn said, smoothly taking a trick.

"It's taken off like a rocket, anyway."

"I just know what she told me."

"What about the last few years, when she stopped playing cards?"

"She never stopped playing cards; she just came less often," Patsy said.

"She became a bit erratic," Evelyn admitted, "but still her bidding was better than—"

Evelyn was interrupted by the sound of flying high heels on the polished wood floor. "Well, hi! Looks like you started without me! God, what a day! You know we've got the painters in and the dog has been sick...."

"This is Anna Peters," Evelyn said. "Lucky you've showed up or we'd be recruiting her for your spot."

"You've missed an experience," Patsy said. "You don't have to go," she added as I laid my cards facedown and started to get up.

"No indeed," said Evelyn.

"It's been fun," I said, "but I've been lucky so far. You better take over," I told Jane Paget.

"I'll see you out," Liz said. "I'm dummy this hand, anyway."

I thanked the others for the game and crossed to the doorway with Liz. "You must think we're awful, just heartless, to be talking about Helena so casually. But we're really not. It's just that none of us wanted to face the fact that she was ill, or that she might have serious problems."

"What exactly was wrong with her?" I asked.

"She had trouble with alcohol, for one thing. I suppose I could say she became an alcoholic, but that's not quite the case. Alcohol was strictly medicinal with Helena. I don't know anyone who enjoyed liquor less."

"She started drinking after she took sick, you mean?"

"I think myself that Helena had MS—or something similar. She was an odd personality. In a quiet way, she was very strong and determined, but she refused to accept the fact that there was anything wrong with her physically. Alcohol helped her ignore what she didn't want to face and gave her an excuse. If she dropped something or lost coordination, she could always say she'd been drinking."

"I've been told she resisted the idea of having a nurse."

"Tooth and nail! But actually, Maria helped her for quite some time. She saw Helena got out more often, took more exercise, kept up with the club. All good for her.''

''And then?''

''Then they had a falling-out and Helena started to go downhill. About six months before the fire, she really did give up cards, kept to herself, stopped wanting to leave their house.''

''Do you know what this falling-out was about?''

''The assumption is that Joe'd been flirting with Maria. I see in the paper that he claims they had an affair.''

''That's the story,'' I said. ''What do you think?''

Liz opened the door to the veranda, saw a large man in golf clothes, and swallowed whatever she might have said. ''I think I'd better get back to the game.''

''Hello, Liz.'' The golfer was big, with heavy shoulders and just the beginning of a paunch, like a football player going to seed. His blunt, strongly modeled face was red from the sun and heat and his knit shirt had dark splotches of sweat under the arms and across the chest. The cleats of his golf shoes grated on the porch floor as he pushed himself away from the rail and came over to talk to us, a beer in hand.

''How are you, Arnold?''

''Surviving. Who's this?'' It was not a friendly inquiry.

''Anna Peters,'' I said.

''Anna's an investigator,'' Liz said. ''She's helping with the inquiries into your mother-in-law's death.''

''No need for inquiries that I can imagine,'' he said. ''That's what we pay the police for.''

"I'd love to talk, but Evelyn will be out breathing fire if I'm not back at the table. Say hi to Sabrina for me, Arnold. Goodbye, Anna. Thanks for the game." Liz opened the door and disappeared inside the club.

"You were around to see Sabrina."

"That's right. Written statements are no substitute for—"

"Don't bother her again," he said heavily.

"Is it a bother to assist in investigating her mother's death?"

"We've had it with investigators. Ditto police, arson squad, and press. The damn insurance investigators are at it now. They come in and next thing you know, my wife's hysterical. I had to get the hell out this morning."

I remembered Sabrina Bach's elegant black warm-up suit. "It's a complicated case."

"Is it? A can of gasoline and kitchen matches—what the hell's complicated about that?"

"It depends who used them, doesn't it?"

"It's clear who used them."

"Then it shouldn't take me too long to finish my inquiries, should it?" I moved to step past him. He had a grip like a gorilla, and I said, "Don't touch me."

"Now, listen," he said, and gave my arm a wrench. I was wearing heels, sensible and low but sharp nonetheless, and I brought one down on the neat perforated leather pattern over his instep.

"Christ!" Arnold said, and let go of my arm to clutch his foot. He had an imaginative vocabulary, and I prudently got myself down the steps and out of his

reach. Behind him, the door opened and Henry, the
steward, looked out at us with professional detachment.

"Maybe some ice, please, Henry," I said, "I think
Mr. Bach has twisted his foot."

"Bad luck before the big tournament," the steward
said blandly.

Arnold Bach curbed his mouth with an effort.
"Henry," he said, "don't let this woman in the club
again."

I FIGURED THAT I could beat Arnold Bach home and so
I drove straight to the Skanes. The side door of the
main house was standing open and a woman with a
clipboard and a man with a camera were standing
chatting just outside. I introduced myself, discovered
that they were from Old State Assurance, and confirmed that Karl Dobin, one of their top investigative
agents, was in charge. I'd met him a number of times
at conferences, and my company had done a program
on personal safety for Old State's midlevel managers.

"He's still in the atrium," the woman said. She had
a sharp, alert face circled by a bushy mass of black hair.
"I'll tell him you're here. We're not authorized to let
anyone else in."

Several minutes later, Karl Dobin appeared, wiping
his hands on a towel. Short, sturdy, and energetic, Karl
affects a brusque, military manner and has a passion
for elaborate checklists and computer-generated forms.
"Hello, Anna. Messy business," he said. "You want
to have a look?"

"Sure. I've been hoping to catch you folks."

"Sign her in, Doris. Peters with an *s*. P-E-T-E-R-S. So, you're working for the defense, right?"

"I said I'd see what I could do."

We walked down a smoke-blackened but intact hallway to what had once been a palatial three-story space with balconies overlooking two sides. "Made a thorough job of it," Karl said. "Near-total loss from our point of view." Far above, blue nylon tarps covered the hole in the roof, and an assortment of plywood sheets closed gaps in the banks of windows that faced the pond to the west and the compound courtyard to the east. A few cracked terra-cotta tubs showed where the indoor trees had grown, and I noticed a few sadly twisted brass birdcages. Plastic and metal chairs had been welded together like strange sculptures and everything smelled of smoke, charred wood, and deconstructed synthetics.

"You'll probably be more interested in the bedroom," Karl said. "I'll be stuck here forever trying to match the fragments to the catalogue."

"Fragments? Of what?"

"They had a notable art collection. Couple of the sculptures are salvageable; the paintings and drawings are all kaput."

"I knew they had a collection. But they didn't hang drawings here, did they?"

"They liked the 'open gallerylike space.' I'm merely quoting."

"An old drawing would have faded in a month in here—paintings, too. This must have been like a solar furnace."

"Oh, they ran the AC day and night, but even with low-ultraviolet glass—"

Our feet crunched on some glass and Karl swore. "Just when I think we've gotten everything." He bent down and picked up the blackened remains of a cracked and distorted picture frame from the debris. "Here, look at this. What do you think this is?"

Most of the paper had been turned to ash by the heat, but one corner remained. Through the soot, I could just make out a pair of booted feet at odd angles and the line of what might be a skirt. There was something vaguely familiar about the image, but I couldn't place it. "A modern drawing," I said. "That's the best I can do."

"We have experts," Karl said. "Let them worry about it."

"Yes," I said, though I had the feeling I'd seen something similar.

"Pictures hung along here," Karl Dobin said.

"Behind the trees? Oddest arrangement I've ever seen."

"Me, too. And the odder thing is that these were investment artworks. Oh, yeah, Mr. Skane was very clear about that. Every one priceless, to hear him tell it."

I looked over his shoulder. "Pretty valuable by the look of your list. But not very well cared for."

"No. That may cost him. Maybe we'll be able to depreciate the value for sun damage or something, offset our other losses."

"A personal policy?"

"Try a million-dollar life. And that's only one of them."

"More than one on Mrs. Skane?"

"Don't say I told you."

"Never. Different beneficiaries?"

"She paid one on herself for her children."

"But the big one?"

"That goes to soothe the pain and suffering of the husband."

"I expect you'll have collected some pretty nice premiums."

"You wish. The policy wasn't much more than a year old."

"Well!"

"Right. So we're fine-tooth-combing this one, let me tell you."

"Prudent anyway with artwork, I'd think."

"With artwork, I check everything twice. It's easy to have an inflated view of artworks."

"Especially when you own them," I said.

"You're right about that."

The northeast corner of the room had been almost completely burned away. "Is this where the fire started, do you think?"

"Yes, ma'am. Right over there. Simple and straightforward. Someone pulled a couple of chairs together near the drapes for those lower windows, poured gasoline over everything, and set it on fire.''

"Quick, of course."

"A minute or two."

"The fire would have blocked the stair?"

"All but instantaneously. You wouldn't have wanted to be anywhere near that stair. Perpetrator ran out one of the main doors is my guess."

"Yes," I agreed, thinking again of Maria's version. "Maybe I ought to take a quick look upstairs."

"What's left of it. Mrs. Skane's room was directly above where the fire was set. See those exposed joists? The only way is to come in from the upstairs corridor. We'll have to go back outside and come around."

"A bit inconvenient," I remarked as we walked down the long corridors.

"Yes, but safe at least. We insisted that all this be shored up before we started working in here. Hue and cry, let me tell you. You figure it: A guy has a million-dollar house, but he doesn't want to pay a few thousand for shoring."

"It's not him walking the joists."

"That's it."

"You wouldn't know which of these rooms was my client's?"

"Now, that I do know. Right here. Police have been through it, of course." He opened the door on a square room with good big windows, a bed, a bureau, a television set, and an ironing board. There were some lighter squares and rectangles on the paper where pictures had been removed. The carpet appeared to have been taken up, as well. I went to the window and confirmed that one could see the atrium and Mrs. Skane's room above, then followed Karl down to the shored-up balcony that led to Mrs. Skane's bedroom.

The fire had run straight up from the curtains and furniture below. The floor was gone and the walls had been reduced to charred timbers. There really wasn't much to see, and Karl handed me a couple of color photos from his packet. They showed an elegant and richly appointed room with what looked to be an antique bed, some beautiful mirrors, and several hundred yards of silk drapery material. "An arsonist's dream."

"She didn't have a chance," Karl agreed.

"And if she'd been able-bodied?"

"Awake and alert instantly—maybe. Asleep, not a prayer. By the time she'd have waked up, it would have been too late even if she'd been a champion sprinter. It was that fast."

I GOT HOME AFTER SIX. The house was dark and there were no good cooking smells. Instead, I found a message on the answering machine: Harry'd stayed late to pull some proofs of the Lem illustrations. Would I buy enough pizza for him and his assistant, Billy, and take it down? Of course, Harry didn't phrase it that way. Artists have two distinct phases, depressive and manic. In the depressive phase, presses break; critics are blind; customers are ignoramuses; and the muse is absent. In the manic mood, the sun shines; the muse bears gifts; and the annoyances of life vanish in the morning mist.

Things must have been looking up around the workshop, because Harry said, "Get a pizza and we'll have a picnic."

I ask you: After a day with assorted Skanes and their entourage, did I feel like a picnic pizza? I felt like a nice hot dinner, preferably cooked by someone else and waiting on the table for me. This was not a generous reaction, but the muse of detection rarely visits her devotees. I went to the phone and ordered a pepperoni and an extra large with sausage and mushrooms from our neighborhood pizzeria, an establishment where I am known only too well. Then I went to change my clothes. Half an hour later, eleven hours since I'd first arrived at work, I rolled up behind Executive Security, Gorgon Antiques, and Helios Workshop.

The workshop smelled of printing ink, paper, and machine oil. Harry and Billy were working at the old handpress, a heavy dark instrument, stark and massive like a piece of modern sculpture. The proofs they'd just pulled were hung on a line with clothespins and my husband and his assistant were deep in a discussion about the precise shade of ink that should be used. The present red was too bright in Harry's opinion, so Billy was laying out some alternatives on a palette.

I set the warm pizza boxes down on a table, along with three cans of beer and a cantaloupe. I'm afraid clever picnic ideas are quite beyond my ken.

"Ah," Harry said after a minute, "here's the food." He touched Billy on the shoulder and nodded in my direction. "We'll just be a minute," he said.

Billy grinned. "'Lo, Anna." He speaks quite clearly, but with an odd guttural accent, unexpected given his dark skin and Caribbean features.

"How are you doing, Billy?" I always have to remind myself to look straight at him so that he can read my lips. Harry relies on body language, lots of gestures, and scribbled notes.

Billy gave the thumbs-up sign and returned to the palette. He was eager for a rather orangy red,• but Harry shook his head, pointing to another color, a sort of greenish khaki. Billy nodded and drew out a streak of red, then added a little blue to it. Harry smiled and nodded enthusiastically and Billy made a rapid notation on a piece of paper before drawing his palette knife across its surface. Harry held up one finger and Billy spread a glob of red printers ink and mixed in a daub of blue.

When it was well blended, he went to dampen the paper while Harry rolled the inked brayer across the etched plate, then wiped the surface clean, leaving ink only in the areas that had been bitten by acid. He laid the plate on the bed of the press, lining up his register marks carefully so that the image would print cleanly. On top, Billy put a sheet of thick rag paper that had already been printed with the first color. Then he layered the three protective felt "blankets" over the paper, adjusting the roller wheel so that the felt pads caught and held the plate firmly. When he was sure everything was ready, he went around to the side of the press and began turning the massive wheel that activated the rollers.

Billy is slight but wiry; the heavy rollers pressed the paper into the etched grooves on the plate as he hauled the wheel down spoke by spoke. I could see that Harry felt a mixture of emotions. My husband has been advised not to do the heavy manual work of printing anymore, and I can see that he hates that. On the other hand, Billy is an excellent worker with a real talent for printing. As his teacher, Harry is proud of his progress, his confidence with the machinery, and his sensitivity to the demands of the medium. Not for the first time, I wondered whether Harry should have had children. I would have been a quite disastrous mother; he might have been an excellent dad.

Billy lifted off the blankets and I stepped over to see the result. It is always exciting to see an early proof come off the press. Billy pulled the sheet from the plate and held it up for Harry's inspection. This was to be the second color on the print; what had been dim and mysterious brownish green shapes were now pulled into forms with the red. Where it overprinted the base color, the red made the shadows and bones of the cadaverous figures crowded around a littered table; where the underlying khaki tone had been stopped out, the red left an ominous fiery glow, the poisonous atmosphere of the Lem city of the future.

Billy's face was radiant. "Right?" he asked Harry.

Harry studied the proof for a moment. "Couldn't be better," he said. "You were right." He tapped the khaki undercolor. "Not too light. That's good color balance."

"The orange would have been too bright," Billy said.

"You've got to allow for the color mixtures," Harry said as he hung the print up to dry. Billy made a note of the shades and hung his color samples up beside the print.

"Tomorrow," said Harry. "Billy's out of school by two. We'll get a batch printed up and be ready to proof the second plate."

"A third color?" I asked.

"An etched plate. The upper world, printed over this."

He looked as if he was itching to start right in, but I reminded him that dinner was ready.

"Oh, you brought two," exclaimed Billy, who can eat a remarkable amount of pizza.

"A pepperoni special for you," I said, and he sat down contentedly before the open box.

"Pressmen need a lot of food," said Harry. "I think this is going to work. I really do." He talked enthusiastically about the prints and about the idiosyncrasies of the press through dinner. I didn't think about the Skanes' burned drawings until we'd finished eating. Billy was cleaning the plate and Harry was moving up and down, studying the row of drying proofs. "I think this catches the smoky quality I want," he remarked, and I said, "I saw a burned drawing today."

"Hmmm?"

"Part of the Skane fire damage. What modern artist does quite realistic drawings? Small feet in little boots, a quite short skirt. The legs were funny, too, set at an odd angle. I couldn't quite place the artist.''

''Balthus, probably.''

''Ah, that sounds right. I believe they owned a Balthus. Who'd handle modern drawings?''

''In this area? I don't know who specializes exactly, but don't you remember Jan sold one recently?''

''Kind of out of his line, isn't it?''

''This came in a furniture shipment from Poland—stuck in a desk or something. The drawing had some damage, but anything by Balthus is rare and quite valuable. I thought I'd mentioned it. Jan was very pleased.''

''So I'd imagine. I'd better ask him if he knew the Skanes.''

SIX

"IT'LL JUST BE A MINUTE, Anna. Jan's on the phone."
Eleanor raised her elegant eyebrows. "High finance."

"What else?"

She rolled her beautifully painted eyes and got up from behind a minuscule Louis XVI desk. Eleanor was in her ethnic mode today: African and Central American textiles worked into a pseudo-Japanese kimono, long shiny black hair pulled back with a Spanish comb, and a great many handsome silver necklaces set with stones.

"Those are nice," I said.

"Like them?"

"Very much."

"I'm trying to convince Jan to back a friend of mine who designs jewelry."

"Great advertising."

"Thanks. You seen our latest?"

"The furniture?" I knew Jan had been touring Eastern Europe again, buying up antiques that had escaped war, rebellion, and want.

"The shipment just arrived from Kraków. Jan's been swearing ever since. You can't imagine how the stuff has been neglected."

"He'll turn a profit," I said as the inner door opened. My husband's business partner came out in a cashmere jacket, a silk shirt, and a beautiful ascot. He looks now like a film star aging gracefully and profitably, but this is only his latest incarnation. Jan Gorgon has been handsome in more ways than I can easily remember. He swaggered over and kissed me on the cheek.

"You're looking well," I said.

"And you, *très charmante*," he said with a flourish. "You've come—no, no, let me guess—to see the Tiepolo? Yes?"

The Tiepolo was a splendid sepia-wash drawing of Bacchus and some devotees that I'd been admiring in his showroom for months. "No," I said, "not this time, though the Tiepolo is marvelous."

"There's another version in the Lehman Collection, but my one, I think, is maybe finer."

"Twice as good. I just don't have even half the Lehman's fortune."

"I never believe in letting money stand in the way of pleasure," Jan said complacently, but I could already see him shifting gears.

"Today's business," I said.

"That is completely different. Excuse us, please, Eleanor. Has she told you? I may have to take on some jewelry to keep her happy." Eleanor winked at me and Jan led the way into his office.

"What can I do for you?" He gestured toward one of his comfortable silk upholstered chairs and sat down himself behind a big ornately carved desk.

"A Balthus drawing," I said. "Harry thought you'd had one a while ago."

"*A Seated Girl*. Very nice, a beautiful drawing."

"Can I ask whom you sold it to?"

"Why do you ask, Anna?"

I explained my interest in the Skanes.

"Poor Mrs. Skane, a lady of true taste and culture."

"A client of yours?"

"Alas, no. Her special interest was drawings, mostly early modern, but some old masters, too. Not really my area."

"But the Balthus?"

"The Balthus, she bought from me." He paused reflectively. "She had . . . not so much a good eye, but a cultivated eye. You understand?"

"Not a natural, but able to learn?"

"Exactly."

"Did she have a favorite dealer?"

"Maybe in New York. She went to auctions, I understand. She mentioned a Sotheby's sale when we were discussing the Balthus."

"What about Joe Skane?"

Jan's broad, handsome face showed distaste. "He is a man I do not like."

"You know him, then?"

Jan gave a little smile. He loves to have inside information and secret, special knowledge. "Yes, I know him."

"I would have guessed a good customer."

"A profitable customer, yes. A good customer, no."

Jan can be almost pedantically precise.

"He is a man for whom beautiful things are just collateral. A Matisse or a Degas is just a more elaborate stock or bond certificate. A very vulgar man."

"That was certainly my impression."

"His only question was, 'Is it liquid?' I ask you, Anna, am I selling petroleum? If not for his wife, I'd have put him out of my shop." He straightened his ascot with a quick graceful gesture.

"So he buys strictly for investment purposes?"

"He buys trash," Jan said, "and some investment pieces—so I've heard, anyway."

"I see."

"There is some talk that he is 'liquefying,' as he would say. Perhaps some pieces will come my way."

"What's still intact," I said.

Jan looked up alertly.

"Quite a number of drawings and paintings were hung in the atrium of the Skanes' home—where the fire started."

"It was my understanding that his purchases were kept in storage."

"Not entirely. Quite a number were hung in the atrium of his home."

Jan scowled and said something half under his breath in Polish. He does business in English and flatters in French; his mother tongue is saved for deep emotion. "Do you know what was lost?"

"The insurance company has a list. I saw only part of it, but several paintings are gone, including a Baldung, and I saw the remains of the Balthus drawing you sold him."

"That man is a crook," Jan said angrily. I was interested that he was so quick and positive. "A crook without taste."

"I'm not entirely sure about taste. His office staff is very decorative, and Maria Rivas is something special."

"Rivas? The nursemaid, whatever she was?"

"Yes, the accused of the moment."

"She was never in the hunt."

"No? Skane claims they had an affair."

"A man who could destroy paintings is capable of anything, but this Maria was an irrelevancy. Joe Skane has had the same mistress for years—years and years. Fidelity is his one redeeming feature."

"And you've seen this woman?"

"Of course. *She's* my client. She likes furniture, ormolu—Boulle especially—and Tiffany lamps, anything large, bright, and expensive. She may have an interesting collection one day. She's an aggressive, vigorous person, though with none of poor Mrs. Skane's distinction."

"Distinction was maybe something Joe Skane could do without."

"Distinction, but not money."

"That was my first thought, but they just opened another Beefeaters; his stock is sky-high."

"Some men are greedy," Jan observed.

"Perhaps. He's certainly the kind you want to think the worst of. I'll keep him in mind. And the lady friend? You haven't mentioned her name."

"Do not say I told you. Her name is Natalie Welsung. She has a nice little house in Georgetown."

I wrote down all the particulars, thanked Jan, and walked back to my office. I sent Martha to the library, then sat down at the computer and tried everything I could think of to check Skane Enterprises, Beefeaters, and Joe Skane personally. I got on the phone and called every broker who'd ever owed me a favor and every reporter who'd ever needed a tip. When I got done, I had to conclude that Joseph Skane was just what he'd claimed to be: a hotshot entrepreneur and developer who'd timed his company's growth precisely right.

Beefeaters is solid gold, everyone said, a high-quality, well-managed chain that gives good value for money. As for the Skanes' extravagant lifestyle, all things are relative. As one of the princes of commerce, Skane could afford to indulge himself.

Skane's obvious solvency suggested that Helena Skane's death might have been a crime of passion after all. When I talked to Lauren Emby later, I was embarrassed by my failure to come up with any alternatives.

"There's a doubt," I said. "That's about all. Certainly, there was money to be gained from Helena Skane's death, maybe a great deal of money. I hadn't realized that she was wealthy in her own right."

"She had money," Emby agreed.

"Could you be a little more specific? What was her estate and how was it left?"

Emby rustled some papers. "Six million in cash, stocks, and bonds; a valuable art collection; some land; two houses—it's a substantial estate."

"And the heirs?"

"The bulk of the liquid assets—four and a half million dollars' worth—to the children. It's part of a family trust. Everything else goes to her husband."

"That's still well over a million dollars' worth to Joe Skane."

"Closer to two million, I'd estimate."

"So that has to be taken into consideration. The fact that the damaged paintings were just recently hung in the atrium is suspicious, as is the fact that Skane's selling off the bulk of his collection. And there's the lady friend."

"You're certain about that?" Emby asked.

"It's all in the land records. Her apartment is owned by Skane Enterprises. She's been a tenant there for the past ten years."

"It gives him a motive, certainly."

"But not a very strong one, considering what we know about his finances and the fact that this is a long-standing affair. To tell you the truth, I've checked everything I can think of; he comes up sound every time."

"I think diminished responsibility is the way we'll have to go. I'm going to see what sort of plea bargain I can work out for Maria. I can see you've been busy, but none of this adds up to much."

I had to agree. The case was like a semispoiled chop:
Nothing was clearly rotten, though it had a kind of off
smell.

WHEN MR. SMITH CALLED, I told him I felt I should
return the check that had arrived that morning.

There was a pause and then he said, "One seventy-
five Park Road. Second-floor apartment."

"Where's this?" I asked.

"Hartford, Connecticut," he replied, and hung up.

I switched on my computer and called up my atlas:
Hartford, Connecticut: population, 139,739; per cap-
ita income $8,238, 25.2 percent below poverty level;
minority population, black—38.89 percent, Hispanic—31.59 percent.

I went to the map file and located the Hartford area.
Park Road ran east to west from near the city center
out through the wealthy suburb of West Hartford. I
knew the Portmans had gone to Florida; that left the
Ceasario sisters the only unaccounted-for staff. Hartford looked to be a likely place, and I dialed directory
assistance and requested a number for Antonia or
Luisa Ceasario at 175 Park Road, Hartford. A moment later, the phone company's homogenized recording spit out the digits.

I dialed; after the phone had rung a long time, a
breathless woman with a heavy Spanish accent answered.

"This is Anna Peters," I said.

"You from the hospital?"

"Hospital? No, I'm calling from Washington, D.C. Am I speaking to Luisa or Antonia Ceasario?"

"I am Luisa. What you want?"

"I'm looking for some information about Maria Rivas. I've been hired to help with her defense."

"I don't know anyone named Maria."

"But you worked together at Joseph Skane's, didn't you? You were employed with Maria for a couple of years."

"You make a mistake. I don't know no Maria."

"She's been charged with murder. I need to speak—" The line went dead, and when I called again, the phone rang unanswered. I wrote out a series of questions for Rosita and had her try, but the phone at 175 Park Road was unresponsive, and a day later, a recording informed me that the Ceasarios' number was "not in service at this time."

I found that odd: People have to have a pretty good reason to disconnect their telephone. And then there was my informant, who raised odd questions, too. Although I didn't exactly believe Tony Skane's claim that the Ceasarios had decamped without a forwarding address, it seemed clear that not too many people would know the whereabouts of a pair of shy immigrant household workers.

If the Ceasarios had information, why hadn't the elusive Mr. Smith come right out and given me their name and address? In fact, why was Mr. Smith elusive in the first place? Was he an enemy of Joseph Skane, trying to stir up some trouble? Or could he be a guilt-stricken family member? I couldn't see any other possibilities, and I tried to think who might help me pick the correct alternative.

The Portmans were supposedly in the Sarasota area. Though Tony Skane said they'd been standoffish with the Hispanic help, that didn't mean they didn't have their eyes open. I didn't know their town, but I knew they had a car. From the Department of Motor Vehicles, I got their registration, and a few calls later, I had both their address and their phone number.

Unfortunately, after this run of luck, the Portmans were not at home—or, like the Ceasarios, declining to answer. I was sure that the cook and the butler were my best bets, but Liz Sisko had been interesting, too. I'd had the feeling at the club that she knew more about the Skanes than she'd found it convenient to mention, and with that thought in mind, I reached for the phone.

I'd about decided that this wasn't my day when she finally came on the line.

"Hello." She sounded harried.

"Is this Liz Sisko?"

"Yes. Who's calling?"

"Hello, Liz. It's Anna Peters. I met you at the Long Hills Cricket Club the other day and I—"

"Oh, yes," she said hastily. "Just a minute." She laid down the receiver and I heard her shouting to someone, then the sound of footsteps and a door slamming. "Sorry," Liz said when she came back on the line. "I have kids out in our pool and I hate to leave them unsupervised."

"Very wise," I said. "I wondered if you'd have some time to talk a little more about Helena Skane."

There was a long pause. "All right," she said at last. "But not here. I've a class at four at the Community College. Do you know where that is?"

"I'll find it."

"There's a little cafeteria on the ground-floor level. Three o'clock, maybe?"

"Fine." I thanked her and hung up.

At ten of three, I was sitting at a stained table with a paper cup of lukewarm, high-caffeine, low-flavor coffee. Some doubtless romantic memory had impelled the cafeteria designer to plump for little round tables and unpadded wire chairs: a faux café look, ill-suited to overloaded students in a stuffy glass-sided box. Around me, tired and rumpled folk gossiped over glasses of diet soda or toiled through inauspicious-looking tomes of math, statistics, and chemistry.

"I'm afraid I've kept you waiting," Liz Sisko said. She came lumbered with a big floppy sketch pad and a plastic bin for art supplies.

"Not at all. I was in the area. I see you paint."

"Something to do," she said. "What a cliché: idle suburban amateur."

"Are you?"

"At the moment, but I'm hoping to lose my amateur status."

"Good luck."

"I'll just get something to drink," Liz said, propping her equipment up against a chair. She came back with a glass of lemonade and a cookie.

"I hope that's better than the coffee."

"Marginally."

"I wanted to ask you a couple of things," I said when she had gotten settled.

"I'm sorry I said anything about Helena that day at the club."

"Why's that?"

"It was probably indiscreet. I don't know anything for sure."

" 'For sure' is what I'm paid to find out. Leads are what I need at the moment."

"You said you'd been hired by Maria Rivas's defense. Who is that, exactly?"

"That's one of the things I'm trying to find out. Do you know a Mr. Smith in the Skanes' circle?"

"No, I don't. What does he look like?"

"I don't know that, either. Mr. Smith communicates by phone or by fax—without return address or number."

Liz looked thoughtful. "What were the other things you wanted to know?"

"That day at the club, you all seemed sure that Joe Skane had asked his wife to put money into his enterprises and been refused. Is that correct?"

"As far as I know, yes."

"When was this?"

"He started Beefeaters about fifteen years ago. He'd had a restaurant in town before that—quite a nice place, but nothing exceptional. It was in the little strip mall across from Penney's."

"How long had he owned the restaurant?"

"I didn't really know them until the Beefeaters chain started up, but I'd guess for quite a while. I think she told me once he'd had a restaurant up in New Jersey before that."

"He'd been in business for some time."

"Oh yes. The big jump, though, was to start the Beefeaters chain. Helena had joined the club by then and we were all pretty friendly. We all had kids at the junior high stage—talk about a bonding experience."

"And he tapped her money to get it going?"

"Right. Not that he wasn't a sound businessman. There was no doubt about that. But they'd always kept her money in investments and for the children. It was largely in trust, anyway. Helena's people were cautious old money."

"But there was no argument about investing in Beefeaters?"

"Apparently not. And it's been a great success."

"I can vouch for that. What interested me, though, was the fact that at some subsequent time, Joe apparently wanted more money than Helena was willing to advance. Was that the situation?"

Liz looked uncomfortable. "She only mentioned it a few times."

"Could you be more specific?"

"Well, you know how people gossip over cards, especially if they've been drinking. . . ."

"How long ago was this?"

"I'd say six years ago, certainly no more than seven."

"And the money was for Beefeaters?"

"Well, we assumed so. She'd say—you know, we'd be talking about the children, their future, and she'd say, 'Joe doesn't agree, but I'm keeping everything in my name for the kids and the grandchildren. The business will just have to expand at its own rate.' "

"So he wanted money to enlarge the business."

"Helena probably did him a favor. He'd have expanded just in time for the stock crash."

"And you're sure she kept to that line?"

"Helena was not a person who changed her mind easily."

I thought about the Skane Corporation reports I'd checked: a steady progression of expansion and restaurant openings throughout the eighties and continuing into the nineties. "Could he have acquired a partner?"

Liz shrugged. "Then he wouldn't have needed any of Helena's money."

"And yet he kept on asking for cash from her?"

"That's what she said."

"Joe Skane apparently had a mistress. Did Helena know that?"

"I think everyone knew that. A long-term affair—no threat to Helena."

"So it couldn't have been a case of sexual jealousy—I mean her refusing to lend him money?"

"I suppose it could have been, though I don't think so. You do have to understand that Helena was not herself over her last few months. She finally stopped going to the club. The rest of us—I'm afraid we didn't visit as much as we should have. I used to go over on Wednesdays before my art classes so I'd have an excuse to leave.'' She looked away. ''I'm sorry about that now.''

''If you went over every Wednesday, you'd have seen Maria, wouldn't you?''

''I saw quite a bit of her, though Helena used to let her have the afternoon off if I was coming. To give her a bit of a break.''

''What did you think of Maria?''

''She's why I decided to see you. I thought she was charming. Very bright and sensitive. I speak a little Spanish. That made quite a difference, I think, in how you saw her. She was shy about her English, unreasonably so, but self-conscious nonetheless.''

''Was she the sort of woman who'd have an affair with Joe Skane?''

''Well, there's no accounting for sexual tastes...but no, I never found that plausible. There's been a lot of talk about Joe, but I think it's mostly hot air. And you obviously know about Natalie. I'm not so sure Helena would have cared what he did, but Natalie sure as hell would have. And then Joe's terribly cheap, you know. He hates to spend anything he doesn't have to—unless it's on himself. Helena used to be a bit embarrassed by what he paid the staff.''

''The Portmans had been with them a long time.''

''They'd worked for Helena's mother. She inherited them, and she paid them herself. The rest of the staff chopped and changed because Joe paid them so little.''

''Though the chauffeur Delano's been there a while.''

"He's paid by the corporation. I think that's the deal. He drives Joe to meetings and that sort of thing, so he comes as a business expense."

"So why did Helena quarrel with Maria? You'd mentioned that she did Helena a lot of good."

"Well, there's Tony, you know. I'm not saying anything definite, but I always thought any disagreement was more apt to be over Tony than over his dad."

"Now that you mention it, Tony does seem to have a somewhat stormy relationship with his fiancée."

"'Fiancée' is a bit of a joke. Helena was bound and determined to see him married. I suppose it was her illness. And then, Tony was never too interested in girls. That worried Helena, too. She could be awfully determined. She liked Susan. She thought Susan could manage Tony and keep him on the straight and narrow."

"And what did the straight and narrow consist of?"

"Law school, a good firm, the right sort of friends. Tony never took any of that very seriously."

"What did Tony take seriously?"

"Well, that's what was odd. He took bursts of—idealism, I suppose you'd say. He'd go off and do good work—soup kitchens or building low-cost housing. He went walking in Nepal with just a backpack. He went off to Arizona one winter. Odd things like that. He visited a Franciscan group out west for a time and then he converted to Catholicism. Helena was quite alarmed."

"What are the other Skanes?"

"Episcopalians, I think. Helena was afraid he might sign on for the priesthood or become a monk or something. I don't know about that. In between times, he seemed thoroughly conventional, probably was."

"An eccentric sort of adolescent rebellion?"

"That was my assumption."

"There are worse."

"Oh yes—but, really, monasteries, gurus, and soup kitchens—Helena's attitude was that they were all right in their place but not for her family."

"Tony's house suggests a healthy materialistic appetite, though."

"Tony used to joke about that. He liked to keep money circulating. He used to call himself the Skane Laundry."

"I see. Suggesting he didn't have much of a relationship with his dad—or was it with his maternal ancestors?"

"Both, I think. He and Joe don't have much in common at the moment. But that might change. The thing is, I think Tony is ambivalent about money. He feels—almost guilt, I think about having a great deal of money. He's never adjusted to the inequities of the world. At the same time, he enjoys nice things."

"It sounds like a modern rationalization for spending and not working."

Liz laughed. "That's too cynical. He's a nice boy. Though Helena was perhaps right: Everything is going to depend on whom he marries."

"Hence Helena's interest in Susan?"

"Right. Susan Langer's totally conventional. She loves the house and nice things; she'll want an ordinary suburban life with a husband and children."

"And Maria? What if she was in the picture?"

"Maria is a different sort altogether. Who knows what Tony'd have become with Maria?"

SEVEN

I CALLED JOE SKANE'S OFFICE just before five and was told that he was out of town. Whether or not that was true, his home phone rang unanswered, so I decided to try Tony Skane instead. The same expensive little sports car was parked in front of the house, and inside, after Hector made apologies that "Mr. Tony" was away, I found the temperamental fiancée.

"You're the detective," she said by way of greeting. She was considerably better-looking in the nontantrum mode: a tall, sturdy, handsome woman with thick red hair and a beautiful complexion.

"That's right. Anna Peters. We didn't get time to meet the other day."

"I'm Susan Langer. I've been engaged to Tony for ages."

"Maybe you can tell me how to get in touch with him."

"Why don't you come sit down," she said, and led the way through to the large and luxurious living room. "Wouldn't you like a drink?"

"I think just some water, please."

She shouted to Hector, who appeared a moment later with a tray. "I thought detectives drank whiskey or beer."

"Not in this heat," I said.

In the ensuing silence, I sat down in a leather chair as soft as butter, fought dehydration, and admired the deep red living room walls that were as shiny as lacquer and probably as expensive. I thought about what Liz Sisko had told me and decided that the impersonal splendor of the room supported her thesis.

"Tony's up in Connecticut," Susan said at last.

"Oh?" That was interesting. "A business trip?"

"A sick friend."

I thought of the Ceasarios and said nothing.

"I got it out of Hector," she continued. "He's such a snob. He never approved of . . . I mean, Hector's always been fond of me."

"When did Tony go to Connecticut?"

"He left on Wednesday."

I had several unpleasant thoughts.

"Does it matter?" she asked, her nonchalance abandoned. "Does it matter?"

"I don't know. Do you know who the sick friend is?"

"It has to be one of the Guatemalans."

"You mean the Ceasario sisters?"

"Whatever their names are," she said.

"Why them? I understood they'd gone, quit, been fired."

"I think they went to the Hartford area."

"I was told they left no forwarding address."

"Tony knew. He speaks good Spanish, you know. He worked in a barrio out west for a while in a recreation program. He was gone nearly a year. I told him there were kids nearer home. There are plenty of children right here in town." I could hear the resentment.

"How long have you known Tony?"

"We grew up together... well, from the time they moved here. We were twelve, I think. We went to the same private school—The Ledges."

I'm suspicious of any outfit that needs an article before its name. "And you've been engaged...how long?"

"It's been an understanding just forever." Her eyes slid away to the collection of old baseballs that ornamented the mantel.

"Sometimes 'understandings' are not as good as plain English."

"Tony just needs to settle down," she said, but I could tell that she was nervous.

"How well did Tony know Maria Rivas?"

"She worked for his mother," Susan said, but she flushed.

"Was he sleeping with her?"

"No. No, of course not. We've been engaged for years." She looked ready to burst into tears.

"He was fond of her, though, wasn't he?"

"Oh, everyone liked her. She was very pleasant; it doesn't mean ..."

"Fond enough so that he quarreled with his mother about her?"

She shook her head angrily.

"Fond enough so that his mother wanted to fire Maria?"

"It was Joe," she said quickly. "Joe was always coming on to Maria."

"That's the story, but I'm not convinced. Besides, Helena Skane must have known her husband's habits. I understand he's had a mistress for years."

Susan gave a rueful little smile. "I didn't think you'd know about Natalie."

"And Helena? Did she know about Natalie, too?"

"Of course, though Natalie was never mentioned by name. Helena never interfered with her and she stayed away from Helena. Well, mostly."

"Mostly?"

"There was some trouble about a year ago. Helena was furious. She said to me, 'That tramp is asking for trouble. After all these years.' That was what bothered her."

I interrupted to ask what Natalie had done.

"She joined the club."

"You mean the Long Hills Cricket Club?"

"No, no, she'd never have tried that. She's a smart woman. No, the club here, Valley Estates. It's part of the total development. An eighteen-hole course, a pool, nothing special, but it runs right past the Skanes' property—almost within sight. Helena just hit the roof. Joe sure got an earful."

"Sounds like the business with Maria was small-time by comparison."

"He did flirt with Maria, though. She hated that. But he knew not to carry it too far."

"So. Helena Skane and Maria did not quarrel over Joe. They quarreled over Tony. Is that right?"

"It was all a mistake, just a big screwup. It didn't mean anything. I told her it would blow over. You know how Tony likes new things. He feels you have to grow, keep growing, keep trying new things and stretching yourself."

I could see that the gospel of growth had not struck her as attractive. She'd been happy right where she was, with matching furniture, decorator design, a supportive future mother-in-law, and unlimited funds.

"Did she threaten to cut off Tony's money?"

"Nothing like that! He had nothing to do with it, nothing at all."

"You mean the fire?"

"I mean everything. It had nothing to do with Tony."

"And Maria? Do you find it plausible that she burned down the house? Particularly if Tony really is a free agent?"

Susan looked unhappy. I think she was basically an honest person, and despite the temper tantrums, she might have been a wise choice for Tony Skane.

"Well?" I asked.

"I thought so at first," she said in a small voice. "I felt terrible about Helena; she'd been like a mother to me. My parents are divorced; mother's been gone and remarried for years. And then ..." She jumped up and flung one of the glasses against the marble mantelpiece. A plate followed. I handed her my glass, but though she took it, she shook her head and set it back down on the table and took a deep breath instead. "And then I was glad," she said, "because I knew

Maria would be blamed. I thought Tony would never forgive her. I thought everything would be all right again.''

"Maria is in jail," I said. "She can't make bail, she speaks to no one, and Tony hasn't been to see her. Isn't everything all right?''

''I thought so, I hoped so. Then there was the accident and Tony just about went out of his mind.''

"Wait a minute—what accident?''

''Up in Hartford. That's all I know.''

''You said a 'sick friend.' ''

''That's what he told me, but it's more than that. Something very sudden. I was here when the phone call came. He went white as a sheet; he was packed and out of the house in half an hour.''

''That doesn't mean the call had to be connected with Maria's case.''

''The only other time he's ever looked that way was when he learned Maria had been arrested.''

I LEFT TONY SKANE'S HOUSE with a lot of ideas, most of them contradictory. I tried Joe Skane again and then returned to the office and began calling Hartford-area hospitals. Antonia Ceasario had been admitted to Hartford Hospital Thursday morning with serious head and internal injuries.

The Hartford police were a bit more forthcoming, especially when they learned that she was a potentially important witness in a capital case. Antonia Ceasario had been the victim of a hit-and-run accident as she was walking to a new job at a local bakery early

Thursday morning. Her injuries were catastrophic, and I had spoken to Luisa just hours before her sister's death.

"Have you had any word from Luisa Ceasario since?" the police officer asked.

"I tried several times to contact her. Then her phone was disconnected."

"It's worse than that," he said. "She's left town, stripped the apartment and vanished."

"Was she employed at the time?"

"Yeah. Local McDonald's."

"Did they have any money? Bank accounts, maybe?"

"Nothing we've found. She left money for her sister's burial, though. Four thousand dollars with a Hispanic funeral parlor in Hartford—cashier's check."

"A lot of money if you're working at McDonald's," I said. "A lot of money to come up with in a hurry."

"So we'd noticed," he said, and hung up.

I FINALLY MADE CONTACT with the Portmans at ten Saturday night. The next afternoon, I stepped outside the Sarasota-Bradenton airport into the brilliant white Florida light. Waves of summer tourists surged through the doors: pale, arriving Northerners stunned with the heat and humidity; parboiled departing vacationers with mouse-eared caps, dangerous burns, and all the evidence of strenuous vacations. It was enough to make me glad I was working.

The Portmans lived twenty minutes from the airport in a solid older home with a tile roof fronting a creek broad enough to be called a river. The Gulf was visible as a glitter under the highway bridge; rampant tropical vegetation shielded the house from the road, the local street, and their neighbors. I parked my car in front of the anchor fence and opened the gate. Behind the screens of the large porch, I could see shadows and the bluish square of a television picture.

"Mr. Portman? Mrs. Portman?"

"That's right," an English voice said.

"Anna Peters. I spoke to you last night from Washington."

"You didn't waste any time," the woman said.

"May I come in?"

"Since you've come all this way," the man said, and unlatched the screen door.

The porch was built of dark wood and heavily shaded by live oaks and shrubbery. Through the screen of leaves and branches, the water in the creek was burning silver. Overhead, a big paddle fan spun the humid air into a muggy breeze. It took a moment before my eyes adjusted. By that time, we'd shaken hands, the Portmans had sat back down on their bamboo chairs, and a large green parrot had perched on the couch and sidled over to take a look at me.

"A beautiful bird," I said.

"That's Barney," Molly Portman said. "Don't put your fingers too near him."

"Bit of a tartar," said her husband. Peter Portman was stocky without being plump. He had longish white hair and a calm, intelligent face reddened by the sun. His wife was thin and straight-backed, one of those impossible people who can look elegant in a loose shirt and pants.

"There's nothing we can tell you about the fire," she said.

"I didn't suppose there was. I know you were out that evening. I wanted to ask about Helena Skane, about what sort of person she was."

"She was a fine person," Molly Portman said decidedly, "a real lady."

"Indeed, indeed," her husband said. "We'd never have stayed otherwise."

"Today, you realize," Molly said, "we could have gone anywhere. A butler trained as Peter was—you can't find them anymore."

"A different world," he agreed, "and different opportunities. Molly and I were lucky. We started out in hard times but we've made a good living."

"Peter was tempted," Molly said. "Peter was tempted by a job near Palm Beach. But I said no. I felt enough was enough, though it would have been a challenge. Theatrical people, they were, a very interesting job."

"Molly reminded me of our age," Peter said cheerfully.

"You'd been with Mrs. Skane a long time, I understand."

"And with her mother before that," Molly said. "What would it have been, Peter?"

"It would have been thirty-two years this month. Five with the old lady and the rest with Mrs. Skane."

"And we were asked to leave on a weekend's notice. You won't believe that," Molly Portman said. "A weekend's notice and an extra month's pay. Just like that."

"Which weekend was this?"

"The weekend after Mrs. Skane was killed."

"Don't forget he parted with that extra month's wages. Half broke his heart, that did."

"Everyone was let go—except for the gardener and the chauffeur, John Delano. Why was that?"

"The house was destroyed. He said there was no work." Molly's voice was dry. "No work except for the cleaning up, the packing, the cataloging for the insurance people." She shrugged. "He didn't seem to care. His attitude was always, 'I've paid for it; it's insured.'"

"He's the kind," Peter said, "that would smoke a cigar and let the ash fall. And they had beautiful light-colored rugs, too."

I was getting used to their somewhat elliptical style. "So someone will have to be hired for the eventual cleanup?"

"That's right. Oh, he'll bring in a commercial firm. See if they don't steal him blind."

"Was letting the staff go just thrift?"

"What do you mean?" Peter asked cautiously.

"I just wondered. He made a clean sweep of everyone who worked in the house. When I started my investigations, it was difficult to find people who had known either Mrs. Skane or Maria well."

"John was still there, wasn't he?"

"Oh, he'd be there, don't you worry about that," Peter said.

"Why do you say he would be?" I asked.

"He's the boss's shadow, isn't he? Mr. Skane doesn't stir far without him, I can tell you."

"He was home the night of the fire, though."

"We've had our doubts about the fire," Molly said.

"Now, there was never anything against the man. A decent-enough fellow," Peter said. "Just the kind that somehow rubs you the wrong way."

"You said you had some doubts about the fire. What did you mean?"

Molly Portman shrugged. "It just didn't seem right. For one thing, Maria claimed to be upstairs. Most nights, if the rest of the house were out, she'd sit down in the atrium so that she'd hear Mrs. Skane."

"Plus, she said she fell asleep early. Maria was a night owl," Peter said. "Took a siesta in the afternoon the way Spanish people do and stayed up half the night."

"She might have set the fire and gone upstairs," I suggested.

Molly momentarily looked as if she could believe that scenario, then shook her head.

"No? Why not?"

"I don't know if Peter was in the house the day it happened, but Maria is terrified of fire. Purely terrified."

"What day?" her husband asked.

"You remember that gas grill they put in the kitchen? I wouldn't have given it houseroom. Sent up a plume like an oil well. Maria was down one day getting something for Mrs. Skane while I was grilling—what was it? Kebabs, that's what it was. They had people in for lunch—Mr. Skane did, I mean; Mrs. Skane was up in her room. I'd just taken off the kebabs and before I could shut off the gas, it flared up—some drippings, you know—and it ignited a paper towel I'd had out to drain the kebabs on.''

"I remember that,'' Peter said. "Right you are. I went for the fire extinguisher.''

"It was all over in a minute, but Maria let out a terrible shriek. Latins tend to be hysterical, you know, and afterward she couldn't even carry the tray upstairs. I was a bit annoyed, to tell the truth, between the goings-on when we had company to prepare for and the grill, which was a menace....''

"They had it taken out and replaced,'' Peter said, "the very next day. Something wrong with the valve; it let out too much gas.''

"And her screaming her head off in Spanish. It was Mr. Tony that told me there'd been a fire back in her own country.''

"Did he say what had happened?''

"Some political trouble, I think it was. He didn't say much....''

"Just enough so that we knew it was nasty.''

"He said we shouldn't blame Maria for being upset. I sent her up some of the raspberry mousse she liked, though I don't know a cook who wouldn't have been annoyed at an upset in her own kitchen.''

"I see." That put Maria's traumatic muteness in another light. "And John Delano?"

"I'd tell a lie if I said there was anything suspicious against him," Peter said.

"Mrs. Skane didn't like him, I can tell you that."

"No?"

"It was a laugh, him staying home that night in case she wanted anything. She'd have been a lot sicker than she was before she'd have ridden anywhere with him."

"Why was that?"

"I don't know, so don't ask me," Molly said. "But she wanted rid of him."

"I heard her tell Mr. Skane several times that John was to go. They had a real set-to over it one night. I could hear them all the way into the pantry," Peter said, "or at least I could hear him. She hardly ever raised her voice. Just the way she was brought up."

Peter seemed set to discuss upper-class child rearing, so I asked, "And what was Joe Skane saying?"

"He was saying John stayed—John 'had to stay,' that was the phrase he used. There's 'no choice in the matter,' he said. 'John stays.'"

"That was rather odd, wasn't it? I assume good chauffeurs are hard to come by, but..."

"I imagine Mr. Skane was telling her *his* mind was made up. He hated to be crossed."

"And was there anything against John? Did he drink, for instance?"

"Not when he was driving," Peter said. "And not much when he wasn't. No, it wasn't drink." He looked doubtful.

"Mrs. Skane was like us. Just didn't like the look of him. Just one of those men you don't feel right about," Molly said.

"He had a lean and hungry look," her husband said.

"Ah."

"He suited Mr. Skane all right."

"But not Mrs. Skane," Molly said. "She had Maria learn to drive so she wouldn't have to rely on John. That's how strongly she felt. And I wouldn't have ridden with Maria for a year's salary."

"Now, she wasn't *that* bad," Peter said. "Though it did take her a while to get the hang of it. She'd never driven, wasn't much used to machinery."

"It sounds," I said, "as if the Skanes were both very determined people."

"They were indeed, but we didn't have very much to do with him," Molly said, "Mrs. Skane ran the house and he ran the business."

"Were they a close family?"

"Close with a dime," Peter said.

"Mrs. Skane was close to the children," Molly said. "They did a lot together before she took sick. Mrs. Skane was always at work. He'd make a show with big birthday parties, expensive weddings and dances—he liked that—but otherwise...."

"Home was for show," her husband said flatly. "When I read the news stories after the fire, I hardly recognized the family."

"Not that there were too many real disagreements—except about John."

"Depends what you call disagreements," her husband said. "Mr. Skane had a bad temper, especially when he was worried. And if something got his goat, he really let you know it. He had a nasty tongue."

"What was he worried about?"

The Portmans sat silent for almost a minute, then Peter spoke. "He worried about money. He was as cheap as they come. That was always true, but he had spells—didn't he, Molly?—of doom and gloom about money."

"Had me go through the household accounts once, top to bottom, the whole year. He was afraid he was being cheated. Peter and I, we were ready to leave."

"Our bags were packed. I told him, I said, 'Mr. Skane, I've been a butler for over thirty years and I've never once had my accounts questioned.' This was over the liquor bill, you understand. Molly handled the food and the other household expenses."

"But when Mrs. Skane asked us to stay..."

"Begged us to stay," Peter said.

"She wasn't too well, poor thing, and she said, 'I don't want to be left alone in the house with strangers.' We'd known her from the time she was a girl. It didn't seem right to leave her with a lot of people who didn't even speak English."

"How long ago was this?" I asked.

"Nine months ago, would you say, Peter?"

"Right. That was in June. They'd just had a big party, that big Beefeaters party."

"A very vulgar affair," Molly said. "Fountains of champagne, that sort of nonsense. It looked like something you'd see in a casino."

"Did Joe Skane ever pressure his wife to loan him money? I mean money for the firm?"

"He would have liked to modify the trust agreements, I know that," Peter answered. "Otherwise, I have my ideas, but I don't like to say. You pick up a lot in these jobs, but a lot of it is just putting two and two together."

"And what about Tony? Did he have money of his own?"

"Oh yes," Molly said. "He got the first of his grandmother's money when he turned eighteen and a yearly income at twenty-one. I hate to criticize the old lady, but it would have been better if he'd had to go to work."

"He'd have had less time to fool around," Peter agreed. "He was always running here and there, one crazy thing after another."

"What sort of crazy things?" I asked.

"Oh, nothing harmful. I don't mean drink and drugs and wild parties."

"No, no, nothing like that with Tony," Molly agreed.

"But he wasn't settled. He was out west coaching a group of Mexican schoolkids. That was all right, but he wasn't a trained teacher. Then he came back and built houses for one of those charitable programs."

"And then the commune or whatever it was," Molly said. "He did that for a while. Lived on vegetables and rice and drank special water."

"Brought a case of it home with him, didn't he? I kept falling over it in the pantry."

"He meant well enough, you know," Molly said.

"But no staying power. He wasn't brought up to work and he didn't really know how. He tried this, that, and the next thing."

"We thought he'd get married once they built the house."

"Not that he took much interest in the house," Peter said.

"No, the girl saw to all that. She and Mrs. Skane helped draw the plans and handled the decoration. A lovely girl."

"The lovely girl, is that Susan Langer?"

"Perfect for him. His mother knew what he needed, but would he listen? Next thing we'd heard, he'd up and gone hiking in Nepal."

"Though," Peter said cautiously as if he hated to contradict his wife, "it's not every man wants his mother to pick his wife."

"'Pick his wife'! Nonsense. They were childhood sweethearts. Cutest things you ever saw."

"Am I right in thinking Tony had another candidate?"

"There was some talk," Molly said, "but as far as I knew, he and Susan were engaged."

"Was the talk about Maria Rivas?" I asked.

"I don't think she'd have been at all suitable," Molly began, but her husband nodded.

"She coached him in Spanish," Peter said. "I used to hear them jabbering away out on the terrace while his mother was taking a nap."

"I don't think there was much more to it than that," Molly said. "But I wouldn't know what Maria was thinking."

"She wasn't friendly?"

"Oh, friendly enough—as friendly as I wanted, anyway," Molly said.

"Was she close to the Ceasario sisters?"

"They all spoke Spanish together. I'm not sure they were really the same type," Peter said. "I think Maria was homesick. Her English was quite good, so she used to take them shopping, that sort of thing."

"Do you think she would have confided in them?"

"Might have done."

"I understand Mrs. Skane wanted to get rid of Maria. I've been wondering if they quarreled about Tony?"

"The papers have been saying they argued about Joe."

"Mr. Skane didn't mean any harm," Peter said.

"He is a rather crude man," Molly said. "You were well not to take anything he said too seriously."

"Was that his wife's attitude?"

"She was pretty philosophical about him," Peter added.

"And about Tony?"

"Tony was a different matter," Molly said. "She wanted to see him settled, married—especially when she believed she was dying."

"I hadn't realized her condition was that serious."

"It may not have been, I don't know. Mrs. Skane was very closemouthed about her medical problems."

"And very reluctant to take medical advice," Peter added. "She liked this homeopath—I think that's what she called him—in Gaithersburg. She saw him pretty regularly."

"Maria suspected a disease like multiple sclerosis."

"She was trained in one of those Latin American hospitals," Molly said. "I'd sooner trust the homeopath."

"And the family? How seriously did they take her illness?"

"Not seriously enough, if you ask me," Molly said. "There's Tony running around and Mr. Skane after her for money and Miss Sabrina with nothing in her head but her tennis lessons and things for the children." She shook her head and so did Peter. The conversation seemed to have run out of steam. In the silence, the parrot tuned up his vocal cords and began repeating his name in a hoarse, self-satisfied tone.

"One last thing," I said. "Joe Skane seems to have been an odd choice for Helena. Everyone gives me the impression that she was much better educated, much more cultured than her husband. Why him?"

"It about broke her mother's heart," Molly said. "But she wanted a man with some energy and ambition. I suppose she was right. Her father, now, was a gentleman.''

''He never lifted a finger,'' Peter put in. ''A lovely old gent, but he couldn't keep up. His brokerage firm kept him on for the name, but I don't think he worked a full day in all the years we knew him.''

''And Joe Skane?''

''Joe's a worker right enough.''

''And a good-looking man,'' his wife added. ''A bit coarse now, but as a young man, he was as handsome as they come.''

EIGHT

I GOT BACK TO WASHINGTON by midafternoon Monday and fought bumper-to-bumper traffic all the way into town. I stopped at the studio to see Harry and arrived at my office just as Martha was closing up.

"Have a good trip?"

"All right. We communicated pretty well once I got used to their style."

"You may have wasted your time," she said. "You've had a call from our Mr. Smith. You're off the case."

"The hell I am!"

"He wants me to figure the final payment and promises the check by return mail. I said you'd been very busy on his behalf."

"You didn't mention where I was."

"Certainly not. Though that's maybe what he had in mind. He went on a bit about wanting to get in touch with you immediately."

"I'll bet. Unfortunately, as far as Mr. Smith is concerned, I got back too late to get the message. Bill him for a full day and include the airfare, but hide it under document search or surveillance or something."

Martha rolled her eyes.

"Be creative," I said. I collected my briefcase and car keys and headed back to the Beltway, where the

evening sun was burning a perfect pink disk through
the smog. The evening crush made halting progress out
to the suburbs before draining away through the green
bedroom communities. I reached the Skane compound just before six. Its green lawns looked lush and,
doubtless, semitoxic, but the main house was still
boarded up, and I could see no signs of work on the
exterior.

The little guard kiosk was empty, so I drove carefully around the loop, avoiding an assortment of toys
and bikes near the Bachs' house, and stopped in front
of Tony Skane's. I got out and put my silk blazer over
my damp shirt. The front door was open, but the outer
screen door was latched. The interior was shaded and
dim, but down the long hallway, I could see two men
silhouetted against the evening light at the back door.

A dishwasher or some other kitchen appliance was
running, but I could hear snatches of their conversation.

"...taken care of."

"I won't have anything to do..."

"...your choice..."

When I pushed the doorbell, they both turned and
one slipped out the back entrance. Dark hair, white
shirt, black slacks—I guessed John Delano. That was
no surprise. What was a surprise was the change in
Tony Skane. He came to the door looking very white
and very nervous.

"We don't allow any solicitors," he said.

"How about private investigators?"

"Oh, Anna Peters, isn't it? I hadn't expected to see you again."

I bet he hadn't. "I need to speak to you for a few minutes."

He made a project out of looking at his large and expensive watch. "It's not really convenient. It's almost dinnertime."

I made a project out of looking back at the drive. "I don't see the sports car," I said. "Or are you expecting other company?"

"Maybe you could call back," he said. "Or phone me in the morning."

"I think I'd better come in, Mr. Smith."

"I don't know," he began, but I was rapidly losing patience.

"It's been a long day," I said. "Don't give me any bullshit. I thought you'd rather I talk to you instead of to your father."

He thought that over, then flipped the latch on the door.

"Thanks. It's good to get out of the heat," I said.

"We can talk in here." Tony opened the door to a little study off the main foyer. "I'll just tell Hector to hold dinner."

I set down my case and looked around the room: A desk and some nondescript chairs sat in front of shelves of paperback books, heavy on sociology, religion, and travel. The walls held rows of photographs: parties and friends, mostly, but also a large picture of the Himalayas and a smaller one of what appeared to be a youth soccer team, with Tony Skane as one of their track-suited coaches. On a shelf above was some Native American pottery, backed by what looked to be a very nice Navajo rug.

"Souvenirs of your stay out west?" I asked when he returned.

He had a couple of bottles of beer in his hand.

"Yeah. Part of what my parents describe as my irresponsible youth. You want something to drink?"

"The beer looks good."

He handed one over and sat down. He still looked pale, but he seemed to have recovered his composure.

"How did you know about Smith?" he asked. "Some sort of tracing device?"

"I didn't *know* until this minute. But you seemed like a good prospect. You'd liked Maria, you knew the Ceasarios, and you probably knew where they went, yet you'd lied about all three."

He looked disappointed. "I thought it would be perfectly safe."

"You hired me for my professional expertise. You should be pleased."

"It's a complicated situation."

"Murder tends to be complicated."

"I was put in the middle," he said.

"Maria's on one side. Who's on the other?"

"Dad tried to make me feel disloyal. The first thing for the family should be discovering the killer, prosecuting the killer."

"I certainly agree with that."

"But the idea that Maria—it was ludicrous."

"But it prevented a potentially awkward investigation?"

"I realized Dad had it in for her."

"Why was that?"

"He doesn't really know how to treat women. Mother, he made an exception for; he was very proper with Mother. To tell you the truth," Tony said reflectively, "I think he was a little bit afraid of Mother. He respected her taste, her manners. Not that he wanted to acquire them himself, you understand."

"I'd gotten that impression."

"He didn't see that Maria was the same type, and when he discovered she was, he was furious. I guess because she was an employee—and not a well-paid one, either. Dad rates money very highly."

"He made a heavy-handed pass at her and got slapped down?"

"That's it—literally."

"How long ago was this?"

"Oh, soon after she came. It blew over. He has a sense of humor, you know. He's not nearly as crude as he pretends to be. And Maria is very clever and efficient. He consoled himself that he was getting a bargain."

"So what was the problem?"

"I fell in love with Maria."

"And your parents weren't happy?"

"Mother was frosted. Dad didn't say much, but I think he resented the fact that Maria preferred me."

"It's been known to happen."

"Then after the fire and all . . . the truth was, Maria refused to see me, refused to speak to me on the phone, wouldn't communicate at all. I didn't know what to think—or who to believe."

"You came up with a compromise."

"I thought she'd accept help if it didn't come from me, and I thought it wouldn't upset Dad as much if I wasn't obviously involved."

"That sounds reasonable. But why have you pulled me off the case?"

"What do you mean?"

"Mr. Smith called again today. I'm fired. Final bill requested."

Tony Skane went very white.

"That wasn't you?"

"No."

"Did you tell anyone about Mr. Smith?"

"No, I did not."

"What about your calls? Make any to me on a cellular phone?"

He thought a minute. "One, I think. At least one."

"You might as well have stood on the corner and shouted. Anyone who's interested can pick up the transmission on a Bearcat scanner."

He looked frightened.

"The next question," I said, "is where were you when you made that call? That might tell us who was listening in."

"I don't know. I probably phoned from my car. I'm sure I did."

I was unconvinced and probably looked it.

"Really," he said. "Who around here would have a receiver and a voice-distortion device? It's crazy. Can you see my sister fooling with anything like that?"

"I've met her husband," I said. "Now there's a different type altogether."

"Arnold's never home during the day," Tony said quickly.

I noticed he didn't feel called upon to defend his brother-in-law's charm and innocence. "In my experience, people are usually murdered by their nearest and dearest—and usually over either sex or money. Given your late mother's age and health, I'm betting on money. Does that suggest anything to you?"

Tony jumped up nervously. "I guess I'm the prime suspect, then. Dad has lots of money; Arnold makes an obscene amount at his insurance company. I'm gainfully unemployed and likely to stay that way."

"I understand you have money of your own."

"I might need more," he said. "If I decide to get married, I will need more money."

"Then it wouldn't have been very clever of you to hire a detective to investigate the arson, would it?"

"People aren't always clever."

"No. Let's forget motive for a minute. Why were you up in Hartford?"

He hesitated, and I said, "Mr. Smith helpfully gave me the Ceasarios' address. I assume that was your Mr. Smith?"

"Luisa called me when her sister got hurt. She was upset, of course, and scared, too."

"Why scared?"

"Well, the money, for one thing—hospital, doctor, ambulance; they're poor people."

"And for the other thing?"

"She thought it was deliberate. She was sure it was."

"The accident?"

"She didn't see the incident, but some of the neighbors did. The car had been parked at the side of the road. When Antonia came out, the driver hit the gas and went straight for her. The car caught her right at the sidewalk. There seems no doubt at all it was deliberate."

"I see." The Hartford police had omitted that detail.

"So you went up north and took them some money."

"All I could do. As it turned out, Antonia was too badly hurt to survive. She was only twenty-three."

"And Luisa's disappeared."

"Naturally. She was terrified. I gave her some money to get out of town; I don't know where she's gone."

Tony Skane was the most unconvincing liar I've ever questioned. "Why did it happen?"

Tony shrugged.

"You must have some ideas. Luisa must have had some ideas."

"Politics, I think. Something political from their home country." He looked at me hopefully.

"Had it happened here, yes, I'd say that was the likely story. But why then, why in Hartford? The Ceasarios weren't politically active, were they?"

"No, no, nothing like that."

"I'd gotten the impression they were simple, hard-working people."

"A lot of people like that wind up dead in Central America," Tony said.

"Undoubtedly. But consider this scenario. Their wealthy employer is killed in a fire, murdered. The Ceasarios' fellow employee and friend is accused of the crime. The whole household staff is immediately discharged. The Ceasarios leave, their destination known to only a few people. A couple of months later, one of them is deliberately run over. What does that suggest to you?"

"Nobody knows who set the fire," Tony said. "Nobody knows, and certainly Luisa and Antonia didn't know."

"Did Maria confide in them?"

"For God's sake, you've been looking into the case! Maria didn't have anything to do with the fire!"

"No, I don't think she did set the fire. But that's instinct; I haven't found anything to support her innocence. And I must tell you, I don't believe much of her statement. There are all kinds of questions about Maria Rivas."

Tony looked uncomfortable but said nothing.

"My question, aside from who did set the fire, is why she was set up to take the blame."

"It didn't have to be planned that way," he said.

Coincidence is always a possibility, but I ignored the idea. "The Ceasarios know something," I said. "They know something or someone thinks they know something. You know that. That's why you helped Luisa get away—even before her sister's funeral.''

"She was in a panic. I couldn't do anything else to help her."

"I need to talk to Luisa," I said. "The sooner the better."

"It's not possible. I don't know where she's gone."

"I don't believe that. Listen, she's got to be in danger. You do see that, don't you?"

"Of course I see that. That's why I gave her the money. But I told her not to tell me where she was going."

"Had you told anyone their Hartford address but me?"

"No," Tony said quickly. "No, no, but it wasn't a secret. There was no reason to keep it a secret then."

"None at all," I agreed. "Did anyone ask about them?"

He shook his head.

"Please, think carefully. Anyone at all? Even casually?"

"No one. Well, no one except John. He worked with them, you know. He asked if they'd found a place in D.C."

"When was this?"

"I don't know. Last week maybe."

"Before or after I spoke with you?"

Tony thought a minute. "After."

"But before the accident?"

"Oh yes, but John wouldn't—couldn't, anyway. He's been around every day. Driving Dad as usual.

More than usual, in fact. Since the fire, Dad's been all on edge. It was a terrible blow to him in spite of...well, in spite of whatever you may have heard. I think it's only now sinking in."

"I'm sure."

"You don't have to be so cynical."

"You're paying me to be cynical. Or am I off the case?"

"Do you think you can clear Maria?"

"I don't know. I've stuck with the case because I'm convinced she didn't set the fire, and I've already come up with enough information to raise some doubts. But what she really needs is a topflight lawyer, someone with more ideas than just the best possible plea bargain."

"We need to find out who set the fire."

"We also need to find out who the phony Mr. Smith is. Do you have any ideas about that?"

"I told you, no."

"Yet you turned quite pale when I mentioned the call."

"It was a shock, that's all."

"Look," I said, taking out my notebook. "Here are the days and times you called me. Try to remember where you were and what phones you were using."

"I phoned from a public phone the first couple of times because there was a booth just outside the shop that had the fax machine. This call..." He paused. "I was here and I think I made it on my cellular phone."

"And where were you?"

"I was outside by the pool. That's right. I'd been swimming. I was going to go in, but Hector was in the house and so was Susan. I thought, Why take chances."

"That was eleven-thirty. Who'd have been on the place at that time?"

"No one, really. Sabrina's at tennis every morning. The children and the nanny would have been at the club swimming. Arnold at work, Dad at work; gardener doesn't come on Tuesdays. And since the insurance investigators have almost finished up, Dad can't see the extra money for security. Guards are on at night, that's all."

"And John Delano?"

He hesitated and thought for a minute. "He must have been washing the car. Tuesday ritual. He takes Dad to work and then brings the car back and washes it before he picks him up at night."

"And that was all—no workmen, no lawn crew, no security guards?"

"You can see for yourself; nothing's been done on the house."

"Yes. Well, what have you decided? Am I employed or not?"

"Let's give it a week," he said. "But don't come here again. I'll call you."

"Call me if you find out where Luisa is," I said.

"What will you do now?" Tony asked.

I didn't feel that it would be a good idea to confide in him. "Go on as I'm doing," I said. "When I get something definite, I'll let you know."

NINE

I WAS BUSY THE NEXT DAY at the office, and it was early afternoon before my doubts about the Skane case surfaced again. There was no real reason to rule out Tony Skane, but his efforts to share the guilt seemed unconvincing. Nonetheless, his chat with John Delano seemed to have shaken him a good deal, and I thought it might be well to find out a little more about Joe Skane's irreplaceable chauffeur, another man who'd had his eye on my client. I got up and went to the outer office to consult with Martha's directory and with her sterling memory; I returned with the number of At Your Service, an employment service that specializes in domestic help and in professional drivers. We had worked for them on occasion, checking out employees for particularly sensitive positions, and I thought that they might have placed Delano with the Skanes.

"Delano," the woman at the agency repeated. "D-E-L-A-N-O?"

"That's right. He went to work for Joseph and Helena Skane about five years ago."

"Oh, yes, the Skanes. Terrible about her, wasn't it?"

"Dreadful."

"We've placed a couple of people there over the years. They never stayed too long."

"Why was that?"

"Off the record, now, low wages. It was kind of a joke around the office. Anyone *she* hired was fine. The old gardener...now, what's his name?"

"Malpas. Andrew is his first name, I think."

"That's right. She hired him and never a complaint."

"He's still there," I said.

"That's what I mean. But if Mr. Skane took them on—six months to a year."

"And John Delano?"

"Not one of ours," she said. "Odd how people will economize with safety."

"Any other agencies around that he might have gone through?"

"Well, none with *our* reputation, but you might try Household Services or Perfection Livery. They handle drivers, mostly commercial, but some private jobs, too."

I thanked her and called the competition. No luck. When I finally tried the state Department of Motor Vehicles, I discovered that John Delano did not hold a livery license, which was doubtless why a firm like At Your Service did not have him on their books. I was thinking about that and about Helena Skane's dislike of him when I saw Mike Garrett come into the outer office with a handsome black man in tow. I waved for them to come in.

"This is Skipper Norris," Mike said. "He just joined us this week."

"Good to have you at Executive Security." The man was even larger at close range and vaguely familiar.

"I'm glad to be here." He had a slight soft drawl. "I'm interested in learning everything I can about the security business."

"Then you're lucky to be working with Mike. He's one of the best in the business—absolutely tops in bodyguard work, protection, and security."

"I'm interested in investigation, too," Skipper said.

"We do that, as well."

"Skipper's just had to retire from the Eagles."

"Of course," I said. "You seemed familiar, but I was sure I'd never met you. You gave my husband a few bad moments this past season."

"Not quite bad enough. We couldn't get by the Redskins."

"And you got hurt, didn't you, in one of those games toward the end of the season?"

"Racked up my left knee," he said. "No more good lateral motion."

"Though good enough for our purposes," Mike said quickly. "The doctor's given him a clean bill of health."

"I'm sorry about your knee, but you're very welcome here."

He acknowledged this with a courtly little bow made more impressive by his great height and weight. "I'd like to be in business for myself eventually," Skipper Norris confided. "I've been part of a team and part of a big organization for a long time. Now I'm about ready to be my own boss."

"I thought the quarterback was the boss," I said.

He winked. "Don't ever tell the coaches that. Anyway, I was a business major in college and I've been looking for something I can learn from the bottom up."

"But not sports-related, and not in Philly. I'm surprised."

"It's better to leave when your time is up," he said. "Too many players hang on and hang on. Security and investigation work looks to me to be a growth industry."

"It certainly is in D.C. I'm sure Mike's told you that despite our small size, we provide a wide variety of services. You should leave here with a pretty good background."

"That's my aim."

"The reason we came in," Mike said, "was to find a surveillance job for him."

"Garrett's showing you no mercy," I told Skipper. "Surveillance separates the serious from the unserious. Highly boring most of the time."

"I imagine a bit like traveling with a football team."

"You may have something there, but I'm sure the food's a lot worse. What was on the list? Anything suitable, Mike?"

"Not really. I don't want to pull Anderson off the Fairbanks case."

"No." I checked the job sheet. It was make work and probably inefficient, but I wasn't ready to give up on the Skane case. Skipper Norris's education was as good an excuse as any. "How about this? For a day or so, I'd like you to keep an eye on Joseph Skane and his chauffeur, John Delano." I opened the file and took out one of the press pictures of Skane. "Delano takes him to work and picks him up every day. I can give you all the addresses, work, apartment, home, girlfriend's address. We're getting a copy of Delano's photo license sent over from Motor Vehicles."

"What do you want to know?" Garrett asked.

"John Delano does not hold a livery license and the late Mrs. Skane not only wished him fired but refused to ride with him. I'd like to know why Joe Skane finds him indispensable."

We talked for a few more minutes and then I walked through the outer office with them and wished Skipper Norris luck. As I was on my way back, Martha reminded me that Rosita's internship was about finished and that I had paperwork to do for her school.

"Say she was super and I'll sign the forms later. Is she in today?"

"I saw her go downstairs."

"Give her a call. I think I'd better see Maria Rivas again while we still have our translator."

WE SAW MARIA in the same bare little interview room with the same tired- and skeptical-looking officer. I thought Maria looked paler and a bit thinner. The police officials had already told me she still wouldn't— or couldn't—speak, so I took out a pad and several pens and laid them on the table in front of her. "I'm sure you remember my associate, Rosita Guzman, who will translate for me if you choose to speak or write in Spanish."

Maria inclined her head gracefully.

I made small talk for a minute about her case and our efforts for her, before I said, "I've been to see Tony Skane again. He seems very concerned about you."

She colored slightly, but her expression was unchanged. "It strikes me that you and Helena Skane would more likely have disagreed over him than over his father. Is that right?"

Maria didn't move.

"I'm sure you understand that if there was nothing between you and Joe Skane, the case against you is very substantially weakened, especially since Tony evidently has money in his own right. There would simply be no motive—or only a very weak one—for you to have set the fire."

She picked up the pen and scribbled. "'I had nothing to do with the fire,'" Rosita translated.

"That was not what I asked you." I glanced at Rosita, who repeated my questions in Spanish, but Maria made no response.

"There's something maybe you don't know," I said. "Your friend Antonia Ceasario was in an accident up in Hartford, a suspicious accident."

Maria was instantly alert. Her lip trembled, but she picked up the pen and wrote a line in Spanish.

"She asks what happened," Rosita told me, "and wants to know how Antonia is."

"It was a hit-and-run," I said, watching her eyes. "Eyewitnesses suggest it was deliberate. Antonia died a day later."

Maria's hands began shaking.

"I'm very sorry," I said.

"Luisa?" appeared on her pad.

"She called Tony Skane and he went up to Hartford. He says he gave her money to get out of town—and for her sister's funeral. I need to know if that sounds likely. Should we believe him?"

Maria Rivas nodded, then put her face in her hands and started to cry. I kept after her but got nothing more, and a few minutes later, the police officer asked us to leave.

In the car, Rosita asked me whether Maria and the Ceasarios had been close friends.

"Friends, yes. How close is a matter of dispute. She spoke Spanish with them, naturally, and I'm told she took them shopping and helped them when English was required. The impression, though, was that it was a case of homesick expatriates sticking together. The Ceasarios were not nearly so well educated or, I gather, so intelligent."

"Yet the only things that have really upset her to talk about are the fire and Antonia's death."

"What about the mention of Tony Skane?"

"She is protecting him," Rosita said very definitely.

"That's what I think. And he, in turn, is trying to protect her."

"Romantic but messy."

"You said it. But there you have it. Just about the time you figure everything runs on self-interest, people will surprise you."

LATE ON FRIDAY, we got an impatient call from the er-satz Mr. Smith with thinly veiled threats of difficulties if I didn't drop the case. I thought that information was worth passing on to Emby. I finally reached him Mon-day afternoon and renewed my plea that he get Ma-ria's trial date delayed. He didn't seem very enthusiastic, and I was working up to an argument with him when Mike Garrett tapped on my open door. I told Emby I hoped he'd consider my suggestion, then hung up.

"Remind me never to work with a lawyer again," I told Garrett. "They're an egotistical bunch of time servers."

Closing the door carefully, Mike moved a chair over next to my desk and sat down, his face intent and se-rious. He laid his notebook and a manila folder on my desk without speaking.

In the years since I hired Mike, I have come to sus-pect that his willingness to take even the most boring routine assignments has less to do with a dislike for office work than with a hope of finding something—or someone. Garrett has always seemed to be on the lookout, a psychological quirk that makes him an ideal, if somewhat overqualified, bodyguard. And though in some ways it is still underutilizing his tal-ents, training new staff has proved a happy compro-mise between his restless anticipation of action and the needs of Executive Security.

"How's Skipper Norris doing?" I asked.

"Well, very well. A nice guy, too. I think he'll be ready when LuBelle gets into town."

"LuBelle?"

"The hot new rap singer. Her manager called. Wants a bodyguard, African-American preferred; wants to check out the arena security firm; wants her hotel room swept for bugs. The usual: full superstar treatment for the nouveau-famous. Skipper'll suit her perfectly."

"Just so he understands the job."

"He'll be ready."

"Good. That's not today's topic, though, is it?"

Garrett took a deep breath. "No."

I waited. I could see that he was excited about something but curiously reluctant to discuss it. He got up, opened the office door, and looked around, then came back inside. His narrow gray eyes ran over the cornices and the baseboard.

"Want to sweep the room, Mike?"

He sat down again, a compact and enigmatic man, his remarkable strength and quickness concealed in a well-knit but unremarkable physique. "We have trouble," he said.

"What kind of trouble?"

"Bad trouble."

"Go on."

"I take Skipper out with me on the Skane job. Piece of cake. We've got the office, the house, the apartment, the girlfriend, right?"

"Right."

He opened his notebook and read from his jottings. "'Thursday morning, subject leaves his temporary residence at the Four Seasons at nine-thirty a.m. and is driven by chauffeur John Delano to the Beefeaters,

Inc., headquarters on K Street. Subject remains in the building until one-thirty p.m., when he walks to lunch with two other Beefeaters employees. Returns at three-oh-seven. Remains in the office until five-thirty, when he is picked up by Delano. Subject is carrying a briefcase and a copy of *The Wall Street Journal.* He is driven to Natalie Welsung's apartment at Sheridan Circle. They arrive at five-fifty-six.' First thing I notice is that our subject sits talking in the car with Delano for ten minutes."

"That's a bit odd."

"Not ordinary executive behavior, anyway. 'At six-oh-six, the subject goes into the Welsung residence. They come out at seven-fifteen, carrying nothing but her handbag....'"

"Tell me what she looks like."

"Welsung? Short, not fat, but certainly not thin. You know, zaftig. Dark reddish hair. Expensive clothes. Bright but not flashy. Attractive for her age, I'd say."

"She's forty."

"Well preserved, then. Vivacious, talking to him a mile a minute. Kind of a glad-hander, too, I'd guess. 'Hiya, John' to the chauffeur—you know the sort."

I nodded. "I didn't mean to interrupt you."

He went back to his notebook. "Where are we? Right. 'They are driven to L'Auberge Chez Francois in Great Falls'—that's off one ninety-three—'where they stay until nine-forty-five. Delano drives back into D.C. to a parking garage on M Street, has dinner alone at the Beefeaters around the corner on Connecticut Avenue.'

When I saw he was there for dinner, I had Skipper go in and have a meal. I figured I'd drive back and make sure our subject and Welsung didn't catch a cab after dinner. But this is what's important. After Skipper's been there about fifteen minutes, he sees the manager come over and say something to Delano. Delano gets up and goes in the back with him. He doesn't return.''

"Delano remains at the restaurant?"

"That's what Skipper thought, but Delano's back to pick the boss up at ten-fifteen. Clearly a prearranged time. He must have left via the back entrance. Skipper felt bad that he'd missed him."

"No, that's interesting information."

"That's what I thought."

"Maybe, though, Delano eats on the house and goes back to sign a chit."

"That's what I thought, too. Anyway…" He glanced down at his notebook and resumed reading. "'Subject and Welsung are driven back to her Georgetown address, where they exit car. Subject is carrying a large briefcase.' Professional courier's model—I'd guess reinforced steel. It looked heavy."

"And he didn't have it when he went out? Was it left in the trunk?"

Garrett smiled. "The next night, same drill. Boss and the lady friend go out to dinner at Jean Louis and a show at the Kennedy Center. Delano drives them there, then to a Beefeaters in Arlington for his own dinner. This time, we wait outside. Delano has his dinner, comes out the back entrance with what looks like the same briefcase, puts it in the car, and goes to pick up the boss.''

"They're skimming off some of the profits."

"Right, but there's more. I pulled a couple of other men and this morning we tailed Delano, not Skane. 'Delano returns to the Skane compound by ten-forty-five a.m. Disappears upstairs to his apartment.' We found a way in through the woods, incidentally. Got a good clear view of his apartment windows.''

I nodded.

"I figure he grabs a nap for an hour or so. All quiet. One o'clock on the nose, he comes down, works in the garage for a few minutes, then heads off to the city. Mr. Delano has an itinerary that takes him to the Panamanian embassy and then downtown. He nips into a parking garage on Eighteenth Street, parks his car, and goes for a late lunch at a steak house on the corner. He gets out of there around three-thirty, picks up his car, and then visits every Beefeaters restaurant in the city. Same drill at every one—we've got the times, addresses.'' He turned his notebook so that I could see the log. "Delano goes to the back door of each restaurant with a reinforced steel briefcase and comes out empty-handed.''

"Cash, you think?"

"What else?"

"Where do you suppose he got it?"

"Two possibilities. He pulled into the embassy; his car was out of sight for ten minutes. That's possibility one. The second possibility is the parking garage. If somebody had a duplicate key, it would be easy enough to transfer the briefcases to his trunk."

"Though it would leave the cash vulnerable until Delano got back."

"If they're doing it that way, they probably change the routine, the garage, the time for every pickup."

"This is terrific, Mike."

"There's something else," he said cautiously.

"Yes?"

"I had the camera with me, of course, and we got some shots. Nothing very clear except for this one." He opened the manila folder and pulled out a grainy photo. I recognized Delano in his dark glasses. With him was a thin dark man in a suit. They were standing at the edge of a sidewalk next to what appeared to be the Skanes' white Mercedes. Mike tapped the second man. "This one is Carlos Ruiz Garcia, 'Charlie G.' in Anglo circles. Colonel Garcia when I knew him."

I studied the photo for a minute. The man had a lean face, curiously sunken on the left side. I looked up from the photo into Mike's fathomless eyes and suddenly understood why some of our clients find him frightening. "Where did you know Garcia?"

"I knew him in Guatemala. You know I worked for Special Forces for a time?"

"I knew you'd taught unarmed combat."

"Colonel Garcia ended my military career—indirectly."

"Personality clash?"

"You could say that."

I waited.

"A friend of mine was 'disappeared,' as they say. Her body showed up near the town dump a month later. I recognized his handiwork."

"How could you be sure?"

"I made it my business to be sure," Mike said bitterly. "But it wasn't too hard. He was fond of fire—cigarette burns, blowtorch. He had an extensive repertoire."

"I'm sorry."

"I wanted to put a bullet in him. My superiors felt I didn't understand 'geopolitical realities.'"

"They can be pretty hard to understand."

"Maybe for Garcia, too. He was excessive even by Guatemalan standards. After I resigned, I picked up work in Panama, guarding nervous American nationals and then some of the locals. I was there a couple of years. Just before I came north, Colonel Garcia, who'd been a thug with a uniform, showed up as Charles Ruiz, international banker and importer."

"A man of many talents."

"A man of very few talents but many clients. Garcia'd gotten himself a job connected with one of the major Panamanian banks." Mike gave a dangerous smile. "He was very careful in Panama. Kept a low profile. Traveled with guards. Later I heard that he was a contact for one of the Colombian cartels."

"Who used to launder some of their profits in Panamanian banks."

"Probably still do."

"Joe Skane's chauffeur has gotten himself some interesting associates. I think we can guess how Beefeaters has expanded so rapidly."

"The sky's the limit with these boys," Mike said.

"The one thing that bothers me is why Skane was after his wife for money. I hadn't mentioned that to you, but over the last couple of years, he'd pressed her a number of times to change the trust agreements and to put more cash into Beefeaters."

"Maybe he began to regret the colonel—once he got to know him better. It's a whole lot easier to get involved with people like Garcia than it is to extricate yourself afterward. And believe me, his business methods would give any normal person pause."

I thought that sounded like a good possibility. "We need to inform the police about this."

"It's much too early," Mike said quickly. I was surprised, because he tends to be conservative and cautious in legal matters. "We need to find out how they are transferring the cash," he explained, "and we need to know if Garcia is the main contact."

"We don't have the operatives for that, Mike, not without pulling in everyone on the staff."

"We can follow Delano for a couple more days to be sure there's a pattern. We can check out the parking garages, that sort of thing."

I shook my head. "This is peripheral to our investigation—important but peripheral. Let me have this photo. I want to know if Maria Rivas ever saw the colonel around the Skanes. Then we'll go to the police."

Mike glanced at the clock. "Kinda late to see her now."

It was 3:50. Rosita, I knew, would already have gone home. "I'll wait until Monday afternoon, but then I want to wrap this up."

He seemed relieved. "We'll have something more definite by then."

His certainty made me uneasy. "I'm not sure I like this, Mike. Personal feelings are always a complication. Maybe you should let Skipper handle the job."

"Skipper's too inexperienced."

"He's impressive, though, and . . ."

"Impressive means nothing with these people; they're absolutely ruthless."

"They're probably a good deal younger, too. Keep that in mind. You and I are further into middle age than we'd like to admit."

Mike leaned over my desk. "This is a favor, Anna, a serious favor. At the very least, we can nail this guy for money laundering, and if he's connected to Beefeaters, Joe Skane's credibility is out the window. Even on the arson case."

"I understand that. What bothers me is the thought of your taking unnecessary risks, for yourself and for the company. I can't allow that. And personal feelings aside, I can't afford it."

"That's why I need to do this job personally. I know how to handle these people."

"Tomorrow afternoon, though, Mike. That's the absolute latest."

His face lightened for just a moment in a tight, eager smile. "Don't think I'll forget this," he said.

"Just be careful. Think of our liability policy." He gave a little wave and was almost at the door when I said, "There's one more thing. The Colonel's expression—has he had a stroke?"

"He wasn't so well protected in Guatemala," Mike said. "He got himself a badly broken jaw and some very poor dental work."

TEN

HARRY CALLED ME shortly after Garrett left. They were proofing the etching plates for the Lem illustrations and lovely things were happening. He was getting all sorts of ideas, and he couldn't say when he'd be home for dinner. I told him we could go out for Chinese. As he described his progress, my eyes drifted to the photo of Mike's mysterious colonel. He was a dark, well-dressed man with a distinctive distortion about his mouth and jaw that was noticeable even in the grainy snap. Combined with what Mike had told me about Garcia's personality, I thought that he would be hard to forget. I also thought that I wouldn't need much Spanish to hand Maria a picture and point.

It was almost 4:30 before Harry hung up. Forty minutes or so out to the jail, twenty minutes to cope with officialdom, a half-hour interview, another half hour back: I had plenty of time and it was foolish to wait.

I put the photo in an envelope, asked Martha to lock up, and left.

I THINK MARIA was surprised to see me so soon, and she glanced at the door as if expecting Rosita.

"Something came up suddenly," I explained. "Rosita had already gone for the day. She's a student and isn't always available."

Maria nodded.

"I have a photograph I'd like you to look at." I put a piece of paper over the colonel's face and set the print down next to the pad and pencil on the table. "Do you recognize this man?" I pointed to Delano.

She nodded and wrote his name on the pad.

"Good. Now I want you to look carefully at someone else's photograph. I want to know if you recognize him and whether or not you ever saw him around any of the Skanes or their staff. All right?"

She nodded again, rather apprehensively.

I slid the paper away from the colonel and watched her eyes. The light was perhaps reflecting off the glossy print, because for a few seconds there was no reaction, then she tilted the photograph slightly and gasped. She opened her mouth, but her lips moved soundlessly, and when she looked up from the photo, I saw her greenish pallor and the thin film of sweat on her forehead.

"You recognize him," I said. There was no doubt.

She swallowed and picked up the pen; her script was as angular and jagged as when she had described the fire. "Colonel Carlos Garcia," she wrote.

"How do you know him?"

"He was known in Guatemala," she wrote.

"A well-known person?"

She shook her head. The angular script moved rapidly across the paper.

"He ran a death squad in your area?"

"Murderer," she wrote.

"Have you seen him since Guatemala? Did you ever see him around the Skanes?"

She seemed frozen in her chair.

"Por favor," I said. "This is important. It might explain Antonia's accident. Have you seen him?"

At the mention of Antonia, her eyes filled with tears; after a very long time, she nodded.

"Where?"

She made a little gesture.

"Please," I said. "Please write it down."

"Party" appeared on the pad.

"A party at the Skanes?"

She nodded.

"How long ago?"

"Eight months maybe. The big party."

I remembered the Portmans' account of the Beefeaters celebration.

"A company party? The Beefeaters party? Where they had the fountain of champagne?"

She nodded.

"Will you tell me what happened?"

She hesitated a moment and then began to write rapidly in Spanish. I could make out the gist of it and guessed at the rest.

"You saw him at the party. You told the Ceasarios. And Mrs. Skane, too?"

She nodded. "Later."

"You told Mrs. Skane later. How much later?"

"A month, two months."

"And what happened?"

She had eloquent shoulders. "She did not believe."

"The Ceasarios believed you but Mrs. Skane did not?"

Another line of Spanish.

"She promised you were wrong? No, she promised you he wouldn't be back? Is that right?"

"She lied," Maria wrote. "He is back."

"And both she and Antonia are dead," I said, watching her eyes. "It's time you were truthful with me. It's time you told me what else you know."

But that was a mistake, because Maria was already out of her seat and gesturing wildly for the officer.

I stood up, irritated with both of us. "Think over what I said, please. I'll come tomorrow with Rosita so we can conduct the interview properly in Spanish."

Out in the parking lot, I looked at the photo again before putting it in my briefcase. The sinister colonel had been at the Skanes' party and in contact with Delano subsequently—which meant that the source of Beefeaters' capital was very likely Latin American drug money. That meant Joe Skane would not have needed money from his late wife—which meant that my client was still very much a suspect.

Turn it around, I thought. Helena Skane had disliked John Delano. From the start? Or since she discovered his link to undesirables like Colonel Garcia? In that case, could the colonel and his friends have decided to eliminate Helena Skane, conveniently blaming the fire on another threat, Maria Rivas? It seemed a bit elaborate, but Antonia Ceasario's accident supported the idea.

If that was the scenario, Luisa Ceasario, Maria, and possibly Tony Skane were all in danger. Maria would have known this, which explained why she had revealed nothing about Colonel Garcia until confronted with the picture.

The theory was very neat, and everything fit perfectly except the actual arson. There was no indication that anyone from outside had been involved. Delano had been looked at carefully, but he'd had a good alibi. I knew there was no physical evidence to connect him with the crime, and the Skane compound was large enough so that his claim to have heard nothing before the fire was well advanced was perfectly plausible.

I was left with the uncomfortable situation that the people with the best motives had the best alibis and the people with the weakest motives had the poorest defense. I reminded myself that my present job was not to solve the Skane arson case but to cast doubt on the evidence against Maria Rivas. That, we could do. I thought I'd better call Tony Skane and tell him so, and warn him about the potential dangers in our discoveries.

I pulled off the road and stopped at a gas station with a public phone booth. The phone at Tony Skane's rang a long time unanswered. I tried again when I got home, at the restaurant as I waited for dinner, and again after admiring the first proofs of the Lem illustrations.

At 10:00 p.m. I reached Hector, who told me that Mr. Tony was out for the evening. I thought Hector sounded nervous, but with his heavy accent, it was hard to be sure. I asked him to have Tony call me as soon as he came in, but I heard nothing that night, and when I tried again bright and early the next morning, I got no response. I put down the receiver and called out to Martha. "What time is Rosita expected in today?"

"Ten, I think."

"Call the jail and tell them I'll be along with Rosita around eleven, would you?"

I decided to get caught up on some of my paperwork, but I had scarcely gotten started when Martha stuck her head in the door. "That's the oddest thing," she said.

"What is?"

"You went to see Maria Rivas yesterday afternoon, didn't you?"

"Yes, I think I mentioned it to you on the way out."

"And no one said anything about her being released?"

"Released? When was this?"

"First thing this morning. Apparently all the paperwork was done yesterday. But there was some sort of delay until her lawyer could be notified."

"Did our Mr. Smith raise her bail?"

"No. A group I've never heard of—the New Hispanic Assistance Society. They went through Arthur G. Leventhal."

"Art's one of the major bondsmen for the area," I said. "See if you can get him on the phone, and I'll try her lawyer."

Lauren Emby sounded as harried as usual when he came on the line. "Bail? She hadn't a penny. That's what I was told, anyway. Though with this case..."

"Somebody made it—to the tune of two hundred thousand dollars' worth. Maria's been released and I'm told that last night she insisted they notify her lawyer."

"I certainly didn't hear from her. Who was the bondsman?"

"Art Leventhal. My secretary's trying to get in touch with him now. Apparently an outfit called the New Hispanic Assistance Society came up with the money."

"Never heard of them."

"Me, neither, but I think we'd better find out a little more about them. Something disturbing has turned up." I gave him an edited account of Garrett's discovery and of Maria's reaction to the photo.

"She'd have been safer in jail."

"That's my feeling. We'd better locate her as soon as possible."

"Have you called the police?"

"Not yet. We'll need to give them something more than just Mike's identification. I'm sure that Carlos Ruiz will have all his documents in order. But we're working on it. It's Maria I'm worried about."

"She must have given an address."

"Martha's trying to get that information now."

"Well, keep me informed," Lauren Emby said sourly. "It's so nice to feel you're on top of things."

I agreed to that and hung up. Martha came in a minute later.

"There was some sort of mix-up," she said. "According to Art Leventhal, Maria was supposed to be met by a member of the New Hispanic Assistance Society upon her release. Instead, Tony Skane picked her up at seven a.m."

"But it was this New Assistance group or whatever they are that raised her bail?"

"Oh yes."

"Better see what you can find out about them. See if they're a registered incorporated charity."

"Right."

"What address did Maria give?"

"She gave Tony Skane's home. It'll all be in the paper tonight."

"The reporters will love that address! Try Tony again while I write a note for Mike. Oh, and you can tell Rosita she doesn't have to hurry coming in today."

"And you'll be..."

"I have some calls to make," I said, "then I'm heading for the Skanes."

I NEVER FOUND the Skane compound welcoming, and that day was no exception. Fall was refusing to come and the day was steamy and overcast, making the boarded-up ruins of the main building look even bleaker than usual. When I parked, I could hear Sabrina's children shouting and playing somewhere behind her house, and the lawn-care men were running a monster mower around the front lawn. I rang the bell at Tony's house and waited a long time before Hector opened the door a couple of inches and said, "Mr. Tony not home."

"It's Anna Peters, Hector. Can I come in?"

"Mr. Tony not home," he repeated.

"I'm aware of that. I'm trying to get in touch with him. Can you tell me where he's gone?"

"I don't know. He not home."

"Is Maria Rivas with him?"

There was a silence and the door opened another few inches, enough to let me see the disapproving expression on Hector's thin tan face.

"He picked her up today, didn't he?"

Hector shrugged.

"Did Mr. Tony pack a bag last night?"

"I don't know where he go."

"But he took luggage? Bags? Suitcases?"

"Suitcases, yes."

"I need to find them," I said. "They may be in danger."

"He no listen," Hector said.

"You warned him, but he wouldn't listen?"

"Nice man but no listen," Hector said.

"That's my impression. Do you know what he took? What kinds of clothes?"

Hector looked as if he was considering this.

"He packed himself?"

Hector nodded.

"Could you find out what he took? It might tell us..." Before I could finish the sentence, there was the sound of a large and powerful car in the drive. Hector closed the door and I turned around, to see Joe Skane's big Mercedes. He jumped out of the car and charged up to the house. He was operating on a full head of steam, because he didn't seem to notice me until he'd let the doorbell ring several times.

"Who the hell are you?" he asked.

"Anna Peters, Executive Security. I spoke to you at your office not long ago."

"Rivas defense," he said, remembering. "She's out; you can pack it in."

"Usually, that's just the start," I said.

"Do you see her around?" He leaned on the bell again and when that did not produce any reaction, he shouted into the intercom. Hector waited until Skane had run through most of his vocabulary before he opened the door.

"Sorry, sorry," he said.

"Where's Tony?"

"Mr. Tony not home," Hector said.

"Jesus Christ! I knew that. Get out of the way." He pushed past Hector and I followed. He looked into the study and the living room, then stamped upstairs to the bedrooms. Tony's bed was neatly made, but the closet doors were open and there was a litter of shoes, boots, and clothing strewn around.

Joe Skane swore and then sat down heavily on the edge of the bed. I looked in the closet and saw lots of nice suits and shirts. The formal clothes had been left behind.

"I knew that bitch was trouble," he said.

"Who runs the New Hispanic Assistance Society?" I asked.

"How the hell would I know? And what are you doing here, anyway?"

"The New Hispanic Assistance Society bailed her out," I said.

I could see this had caught his attention. "Another one of those crackpot civil rights groups?"

"Unregistered. No one in the Hispanic community's ever heard of them. Any other thoughts?"

"Other than my crazy son, you mean?"

"It wasn't Tony. Maria apparently panicked when she heard she'd been bailed. Demanded a call to her lawyer, insisted she make it herself."

"I thought you said she couldn't speak."

"She can't. And I don't think she's faking, because the call was evidently terribly important. I spoke to the police officer this morning: Maria got on the phone, couldn't speak, and began to cry. The officer took the receiver, identified herself, and the party hung up."

"So?"

"So Tony picked her up before seven this morning. When the New Hispanic Assistance Society representative arrived at nine, Maria was nowhere to be found. Everyone agrees that this is a woman with nice manners, but she gets two hundred thousand dollars' bail raised and doesn't even stick around to say thank you. What does that suggest?"

"The woman's crazy, loony. I told you that the first time you came into my office. Right? She's certifiable."

"She's scared. And she has her reasons. You remember Antonia Ceasario, don't you?"

"Ceasario? Sure. She was the little one. She and her sister worked for us."

"Antonia was killed in a hit-and-run accident up in Connecticut. The best guess there is is that she was murdered. Luisa disappeared immediately afterward."

I thought Joe Skane had begun to look uneasy. "You know these Latins," he said.

"Tony's been up in Connecticut. He says he paid for Antonia's funeral and gave Luisa money to leave town."

Joe Skane threw up his hands. "That's the sort of cheese-brained thing he'd do."

"Would he? Some people might like him for the hit-and-run driver."

"Not Tony," Joe said quickly, and I thought better of him.

"Why not? He's going to profit from his mother's death. He told me himself he will need more income if he wants to get married. Both you and his mother disapproved of his relationship with Maria. And if he was involved in the fire, the Ceasarios might well have known about it. How does that sound?"

"The dumbest thing I've ever heard. You don't know Tony. He's not tough. Tony wants to smell the flowers. He's a useless damn kid."

"Someone else set the fire?"

"That damn Maria," Joe said, but without much heat.

"Maria was all set to take the blame. She was awaiting trial; justice was to be served. Then all of a sudden someone wanted her out of jail, pronto. Who could that be?"

Skane jumped up and began moving restlessly around his son's room, picking up a discarded tie, peering at the snapshots pinned to the wall, fiddling with the window curtain.

"Someone with a lot of money," I suggested.

"Don't look at me," he said. "Hey, I'm a reasonable, generous guy, but I draw the line at anyone who hurts my family. I'd have let her rot there."

"I'd gathered that was your idea."

He began pounding a fist into his palm.

"How much do you know about your chauffeur, John Delano?"

Skane got very still; when he turned around, the bluster was gone and something hard and dangerous had appeared in its place. I saw that I might have underestimated him.

"What's your interest in John?"

"He has some usual duties for a chauffeur and he has some fascinating friends."

"I didn't ask you what you knew about him; I asked you what your interest was."

"I'm interested in anything to do with your wife's death. Your wife didn't like him. I began to wonder why."

"And what did you find out?" he asked.

"I found out that she probably had good reasons."

"Helena was temperamental," he said.

"John Delano has some very undesirable contacts. You should check them out. Because I think they're after Maria, and if Tony's with her, he's in danger. Keep that in mind."

"Who? Who are you talking about?" he asked irritably. I had the feeling that he both did and didn't know.

"The New Hispanic Assistance Society," I said. "Who else?"

"I told you I've never heard of them."

"Better think again," I said. "This is your son's life we're talking about."

"None of this would have happened if you hadn't started snooping around," he shouted, jumping to his feet and pacing angrily around the room. "If anything happens to Tony, it's your fault entirely. Jesus Christ, I don't see how I can be blamed for this. That's what happens in this society: Make a success of something and everybody's on your tail."

"They're not financing my restaurants," I said.

"Be careful what you say about Beefeaters or I'll have you in court for libel. Our name's solid gold and I'll see it's protected. I'll have your license," Joe said. He was a man who ran to shouting and stamping, but beneath the bluster, I was sure he was nervous.

"I might have proof," I said. "Gathering evidence is my business."

"If you had proof, it would be on the table and we'd be talking cash. Listen, there're crazy people everywhere. But business is business. The other stuff, politics, probably—I don't get involved in that. Tony, either; Tony doesn't know anything about politics."

"But I'm told Maria does," I said. "And maybe you'd better learn. Your wife knew, didn't she?"

"What are you talking about?"

"At some point, your wife refused to loan you any more money. Was that because she didn't trust your associates?"

"You know a great deal, don't you?"

"Enough to know that the case against Maria Rivas is full of holes. But I'm not really interested in your affairs. I want to find the people behind this New Hispanic Assistance Society, and I want to find Tony and Maria."

"What I want is for you to get the fuck out of here right now. I'll find Tony. And when I do, he'll get a piece of my mind he won't forget. Now get out of my house."

"Suit yourself," I said, and headed for the door. Joe accompanied me with a list of threats and demands that extended as far as the front hall.

"Nice talking to you," I said. Behind me, the door almost rattled off its hinges and I could hear Joe shifting his focus to Hector.

I crossed the gravel to my car, then drove around the loop and out to the road. As I checked the oncoming traffic on the main road, I remembered Mike Garrett mentioning "a way in through the woods." I took the next turn back into the development and spent a good quarter of an hour driving around a serpentine tangle of streets with names like Cliffside Court and Briarwood Road. On Fox Run Lane, I found a dirt track leading to a homesite that had been nipped in the clearing by the recession. I turned in, pulled my car behind a pile of decaying logs and brush, and got out.

To the best of my reckoning, I was somewhere to the northwest of the Skane property. I opened my trunk, took out the sneakers I keep in the car, and tucked my slacks into the top of my socks to keep out ticks. I locked my purse and briefcase in the back, put my lightweight binoculars in my pocket, and started walking through the woods. There was a rise to my left, and I clambered up a rocky outcrop, keeping one eye open for snakes. At the top, I had a surprisingly good view of the development's expensive slate and tile roofs, its swimming pools, ponds, tennis courts, and its eighteen-hole golf course.

The Skanes' colossal main house was perhaps three hundred yards away, and I saw now that I could have saved myself a nasty scramble by walking down the fairway that ran directly behind their property. My present route looked less appealing, but if I pushed my way through the brush below the rocky ledges, I would be able to get quite close to the garage and the garden.

The slope turned out to be a good deal steeper, rockier, and bushier than I'd anticipated. It was slow going, and during my progress, I made a large warm-blooded target for the flies and mosquitoes of the area. Finally, I reached an open woodlot with a tasteful understory planting of azaleas. I walked to the edge of the lawn, picked a spot where I could see the drive and the garage, and sat down behind a rhododendron to wait.

Twenty minutes later, I heard a car start up and trained my binoculars on the driveway. Skane's big white Mercedes rolled around the drive and stopped in front of the garage and tooted. A door opened and closed, then the car pulled away and I saw Delano walking back to the garage. I waited another five minutes before making my way through the trees to Tony Skane's house. The rear of the building had a good-sized stone terrace and a pool that was screened by boxwood and dogwoods and closed off by a fence. I walked quickly around the pool, crossed the terrace, and tried the locked back door, then tapped on the glass.

A shadow moved in the kitchen beyond. "Hector."

He opened the door and motioned me in silently.

"Delano's still in the garage," I said. "Be careful of him."

"What you want?"

"I want to know where Tony went. Did he take his car?"

Hector nodded.

"Did he call an airline? Or Amtrak maybe?"

"He call two, three airline."

"Looking for reservations probably."

"For two."

"Reservations for two people?"

Hector nodded.

"Do you know where he wanted to go?"

"He did not say."

"I noticed his good clothes, his suits and dress shoes, were still in the closet. What did he pack?"

"Jeans, hiking boots."

"Any warm clothing? Sweaters?"

Hector thought a moment. "One sweatshirt, no more."

"Somewhere in the country, I think."

Hector nodded. "No city clothes."

"Where does he go on vacation?"

"All over. Maine, Caribbean, out west, California."

"If Maria's with him, I don't think they'll risk leaving the country. Can you think of any hotels he might stay in? Does he have an address book?"

Hector was considering this when I heard the sound of a key in the front door. Hector grabbed my arm. The big modern kitchen was an open plan, clean and efficient, with no convenient exit, no little closet or butler's pantry. Hector opened a tall, narrow cabinet. An ironing board dropped down and as footsteps came along the hall, I stepped between the door and the wall. I had just enough time to notice that the door ended a good six inches above the floor when something heavy and metallic was placed on the kitchen table.

"The boss is not happy," John Delano said.

"Sorry," said Hector.

I could hear water running and then he came over to the ironing board and plugged in an iron. I heard the rustle of cloth and the creak of a wicker laundry basket.

"What's all this?"

I thought I was discovered for sure and took a deep breath, but Hector spoke up.

"I work," he said. "Whether Mr. Tony here or not."

A chair or a stool was pulled across the floor and I heard Delano sit down.

"Waste of time," he said. "He's not coming back for those shirts."

Hector began ironing vigorously, too vigorously. The ironing board vibrated slightly, rocking the cabinet door back against my shoulder.

"How you know?" Hector asked.

"Common sense. Mr. Tony should never have left."

"He be back," Hector said.

"That depends."

"On what depends?"

"On who finds him. The boss is of two minds."

"The boss not hurt Mr. Tony."

"He's counting on that, is he? That's a mistake. You tell Mr. Tony when he calls that he's making a mistake. He was warned to keep out of this. I warned him myself. I told him it was all taken care of." Delano spoke in a regretful tone. "I don't like people who won't listen."

"Some people talk too much."

The chair scraped back and I heard Delano stand up. "Yeah. And some don't talk enough."

The iron hissed as Hector set it down on the board. "I tell boss I don't know where Tony is."

"Yeah, that's what you told the boss. Try to tell me something different."

"He left before breakfast."

"And then?"

"He no come back."

There was a sound, the iron bounced onto the floor, and Hector got slammed into the board. I could hear their breathing and the sound of blows. I pushed the door, but it was blocked by the ironing board.

"I don't know!" Hector's voice was shrill and pained. Another thump and a gasp, then the mechanical click of a spring catch and the board swung back up into its housing. Delano's hand had gotten caught in the mechanism, I think, because he began swearing. Around the corner of the door, I saw Delano's dark shirt and Hector with blood on his face. There was something in Delano's hand. Before I could hesitate, I shoved back the cabinet door, picked up the iron and slammed the hot metal into the back of his head.

He was a bit taller than I'd figured and I didn't hit him solidly enough. He let out a shout and started to turn, but Hector dove at him. With this distraction, I hefted the iron again and took better aim. Delano gave a little coughing sigh and sank to the floor with his .38.

"Son bitch," Hector said.

"You said it." My arm was beginning to tremble and I set the iron down. I reached into Delano's pants pocket and hauled up his keys. "No reason for him to have a key for this place."

Hector unfastened the key and slipped it into his pocket. Then he went over to the sink, turned on the cold water, and began washing his bleeding mouth. "Do you want me to call the police?" I asked.

"No police," Hector said quickly. "No police."

"There'll be trouble when he wakes up."

"No police. I fix." He grabbed Delano's arms and dragged him out into the hall. Delano was already beginning to make little groggy sounds. "Open door, please."

The door led to a large, tidy basement. Hector unceremoniously dragged Delano downstairs and left him. "Door locks," he said when he returned.

"And when he gets out?"

"We go now," Hector said.

"I want to look in the study," I said. "That's where Tony'd have called the airlines from, isn't it?"

Hector nodded.

The study did not seem promising initially. There were a couple of newspapers on the desk and several books piled on the floor beside a chair, but I couldn't find an address book and there were no slips of paper, no scribbled notes. "Has the basket been emptied?"

"Not today." Hector lifted the basket onto the table and I tipped out the contents—a couple of candy wrappers, junk mail, a couple of used tissues. Nothing. I looked around the room: Navajo rug, pottery, photo of the soccer team—brown faces, black shorts, and red shirts with DUST DEVILS in white script.

"Ah," said Hector. He was holding up a computer-generated promise of a million-dollar sweepstakes win. Scribbled on the back were a series of times: 9:05, 9:56, 10:40, 1:30; 10:15, 11:05, 12:40, 2:30; 3:15, 4:05, 5:40, 7:30.

"Thank you, Hector."

"Very welcome," he said. "I need ride to town."

"I hope you don't mind a walk in the woods first," I said.

ELEVEN

WHEN I GOT BACK to the office, I gave Martha the list of times Hector had found. "Try domestic flights," I told her, "Maybe heading west." Half an hour later, she came into my office and announced success.

"That's provided we assume the second time is central time and the third is mountain."

"Nothing else works?"

"No. With that assumption, we've got Dulles to O'Hare to Phoenix."

"And Tony Skane worked in Arizona and has friends there. That sounds promising. See if you can get me on a flight into Phoenix tonight or tomorrow."

Martha went out to make my reservations and I phoned Molly Portman again. I heard a good deal about Tony's work out west, but nothing very specific as to locale. "They were all Mexican boys," she said, "and there was a priest involved. Father something or other, that's all Tony ever called him."

"But you don't remember the city?"

"I think it was a pretty small place. He always said how hot it was. That's all I remember. And pictures of cactus. Peter probably still has them—he saves things like that—but we're not really unpacked yet and goodness knows where Peter's scrapbooks might be."

I thanked her for her trouble, asked her to call if she or Peter did remember anything, and moved on to the rest of my list. Susan Langer, engaged to Tony "for ages," was my best bet, and though it seemed a shame to bring up her eloping fiancé, I decided I didn't have much choice.

She sounded quite different on the phone, very cool and controlled. "Yes, I remember our conversation," she said when I'd introduced myself.

"I'm trying to locate the community organizer Tony Skane worked for out in Arizona."

She took her time about answering. "What an odd thing to want to know."

"Not at all," I said as brightly as I could manage. "One of our witnesses has suddenly moved away from Connecticut. She's a devout Catholic, and I thought that might just be the place Tony would recommend."

"Why don't you ask Tony yourself?"

"I haven't been able to get in touch with him. I believe he's away for a few days. Hector said something about—"

"He's gone, hasn't he?" She had a disconcerting way of ignoring crucial issues and then pouncing on them.

"Hector? No, I don't think so."

"Tony," she said very distinctly. "Tony's run off."

"I think he's taking a holiday," I said.

"I haven't been able to get a thing out of Hector."

"I think he's to have a few days off, as well."

"He's gone with that woman, hasn't he?"

"I don't know for sure," I said, "but it is important that I locate him."

"Just like his father. I should have known though they're so different, night and day, but it's true. Women turn out like their mothers and men like their fathers."

"I need to find Tony," I repeated. "The sooner the better."

"Why did he do it?" she asked, her self-control beginning to fray around the edges.

"I don't know and I'm not apt to know until I find him."

"He can go to hell," she said.

"Maria will still be in a whole lot of trouble," I suggested, but Susan Langer was beyond such easy consolations.

"I don't care," she said.

"Don't you care if Tony's safe or not?"

"I don't care if he's alive or not," she said, and slammed down the receiver.

My other contacts produced no better results. Arizona is a big state and a Father something or other and a youth soccer team were not going to narrow the search very much. I was not in a particularly good mood when five o'clock approached and Mike was nowhere to be found.

"What's on the log?" I asked Martha.

"Just 'Skane case.'"

"He knows I want this wrapped up and turned over to the police," I said.

"He may have been stuck in traffic."

"He's gone off on a tangent. It's that damn colonel." I fiddled with our radio and managed to raise Skipper. He called me back from a public phone five minutes later.

"Where are you?" I asked.

"Outside the Beefeaters headquarters. I've been waiting for Delano to pick up his boss."

"You'll wait a while longer," I said. "Delano's locked in Tony Skane's basement, but don't let on you know that."

"That explains why he's late. Delano's usually very punctual."

"Where's Mike?"

"He's supposed to meet me here by five."

"Where is he now?"

"I'm not sure," Skipper said cautiously.

"He's keeping an eye on the colonel, isn't he? He's to get off that entirely. I'm going out of town, and I want everything you've found to be turned over to the police. Tell Mike I'll wait at the office until I hear from him."

"Right," said Skipper.

The call came at close to six, and the delay hadn't improved my disposition. "The colonel's been looking for Delano, and he showed up at Skane's office just at quitting time," Mike said. I could hear the excitement in his voice, a thin vein of danger and interest buried under professional detachment. "These boys are very close."

"Where is he now?"

"Still upstairs."

"Leave him there. Finding out where Delano is will give them some exercise. You and Skipper get the report written up and turn it over to the police. Maybe send a copy to Immigration, too."

"We can photograph him and Skane together. I know we can."

"We don't need that. And at the moment, I don't want unnecessary pressure on Skane—or your colonel. Our first priority is to find our client and Tony Skane before someone else does."

"Listen, Anna, this guy is a bona fide psychopath. If we can show Skane knows him—hell, anyone who looks at his record is going to think twice about that arson."

"He's been in contact with the chauffeur; he was at the Skanes' big Beefeaters party—Maria saw him there and probably the Ceasarios did, too. We've got plenty, and I want you and Skipper off the surveillance right now."

We went back and forth on this for a few minutes, until I had to remind Mike that his time was money and that we had other jobs on the line. I was thoroughly annoyed by the time he gave a grudging and, probably insincere, assent. As insurance, I sat down at my computer and typed out a brief memo. I put the memo with the photo of Delano and the colonel in an envelope addressed to a D.C. police detective I knew and left it in the out basket for Martha. Then I put out the lights, armed the overnight security system, and went downstairs.

Our area has looked up in the last few years and, as
a consequence, our converted old warehouse has acquired a variety of new neighbors. The parking lot is
closed in now on all sides, accessible by an alleyway
just broad enough to take Jan's delivery trucks. Normally by this hour, Jan's van is the only vehicle left
besides my car, but when I opened the door, the first
thing I noticed was a maroon Ford with its engine running.

I stopped with the back door partly open. A work-
man for Jan? A late delivery? Caterers for a gallery re-
ception? I was about to step outside and ask when I
registered that the slight figure in the driver's seat had
a curious and inappropriate smile, that he was barely
in his teens, that he had something in his hand. I pivoted against the heavy door and ducked back inside.
I'm going to feel awfully foolish, I thought, just as a
ferocious clatter hit the reinforced steel and chewed
into the doorframe. I dropped flat to the floor, my ears
ringing and my heart jumping.

In the momentary silence, the thought came that I
had unlocked the door and that it was only a few steps
from the car to the entry. I had just scrambled up to
check the lock when a second volley crashed against the
building. The security alarm began to wail and, in between the bursts of sound, I heard a car engine roar. I
opened the door a crack. The car was silhouetted
against the afternoon light at the head of the alley for
a moment, but though I rushed onto the stoop, I could
not catch the plate, and later I had to tell the patrol-

man I could remember nothing beyond the make and the color.

"No idea of the model? Two-door, four-door?"

"I'm sorry. It happened so fast. I saw the car, I knew it shouldn't be there, and I was going out to see what he wanted when—I don't know what alerted me."

"You saw the weapon maybe?" The policeman had been right at the end of his shift and even the excitements of a near homicide didn't seem to console him for the delay.

"I saw him raise his hand," I said. The very thought brought back the light and dark pattern of the parking lot, the sticky heat, the panicky animal sense of something wrong. "With all the news about those drive-by shootings, I was nervous. I guess."

Beside me, Jan cleared his throat. He managed to give it a highly skeptical inflection. In the minutes before the police arrived, I had given him a condensed and doubtless unsatisfactory summary of the present situation, ending with the reasons why I had to be on the plane to Phoenix the next morning. I was not entirely sure he would go along with my ideas.

"Odd MO for a burglary," the patrolman observed.

"What else?" I asked. "Mr. Gorgon has a very extensive and valuable inventory."

"That right, sir?"

Jan's inventory was his weak spot. "I have one of the best collections of artworks and antiques in the city—maybe in the entire East."

The patrolman dutifully made a note on his pad, then glanced again at the dented and pitted door. He was clearly thinking, as I would have, that it was the stupidest possible way to break into a building.

"He seemed very young," I said, "a teenaged boy."

"It's the kids that like these big-caliber weapons," the patrolman said. We discussed the younger generation for a few minutes and contributed "what is the world coming to" noises. I was beginning to feel sick to my stomach and my head kept pounding in a steady and disagreeable rhythm.

"We'll be in touch," the patrolman concluded; Jan and I thanked him and said good night.

"You look like a dead fish," Jan said when the door closed.

"I'm lucky not to be a dead fish."

"You have a drink," Jan said. He is a profound believer in the sovereign properties of genuine Polish vodka.

"I don't think my stomach would take it, Jan."

"Nonsense. You come have a drink and tell me why I have to replace the rear door."

"You must admit that reinforced model was worth every penny."

"Only if one rents to a security firm."

"Now, we don't know that he was after me."

"But we can guess," Jan said, holding open the door of his office. "Sit down."

I sat down on one of his pretty apricot silk chairs and obediently took the crystal shot glass filled with liquid

anesthetic. It felt unnaturally heavy in my hand just as
the muscles of my arm felt unnaturally weak and the air
conditioning unnaturally cold.

"I'll drive you home," he said.

"No, no, Harry will wonder; I don't want him worried." The vodka had a cold medicinal burn.

"He has to be told," Jan exclaimed. "Suppose your
friend with the semiautomatic comes back? Everyone
has to be told."

I knew this was true, if unwelcome, and reluctantly
my brain began functioning again. "We can close off
the alley for a couple of days. Just put up a heavy saw-
horse and a repair notice. Keep people from driving
right in."

"Better you should rethink your present clientele,"
Jan said.

"Believe me, I am. And I've left a note for Martha
to mail to the D.C. police tomorrow. But I've got to get
out to Arizona before some other crazy finds my client." I stood up and discovered that the general un-
easiness in my digestive tract had been replaced by an
uncertainty of perception.

"I'll drive you home," Jan said again, and this time
I agreed. We were on our way out when the phone rang
in my office. Normally, I would have let it ring, but I
was glad for any excuse to delay opening the rear door
again and stepping out into the parking lot. I fumbled
for my keys, unlocked the office, and picked up the
phone.

"Executive Security, Anna Peters speaking."

"Tucson," a hoarse voice said.

"Is that Susan Langer? Are you all right?"

"Tucson," she repeated, and hung up.

TWELVE

A LINE OF THUNDERSTORMS made us late out of Dulles and I missed my connection in Chicago. I waited around a couple of hours, got on a flight to Dallas, and finally got on a Phoenix plane that brought me in as the sun was setting. I hoped that whoever else was on Tony and Maria's trail had made equally lousy connections.

As I drove south through the desert to Tucson, I attempted to forget about yesterday's gunfire and a nervous argument with Harry and to concentrate on the positives. Mike and Skipper had discovered enough to raise all kinds of questions, and the D.C. police might even now be preparing to question the colonel, Delano, and possibly the president and CEO of Beefeaters. With these pleasing thoughts in mind, I slept the sleep of the just at an unpretentious motel. Early the next morning, I drove to the Tucson *Citizen,* armed with the photo of the Dust Devils soccer team and a vague description of a Catholic charitable organization.

"Someone in sports maybe," the receptionist said. Her white blond hair and shocking pink lipstick made a vivid contrast against her deep tan. She pushed a series of buttons and summoned a tall, thin, slow-moving man who adjusted a pair of little round glasses and examined the soccer photo closely. It struck me that my informants are looking younger and younger these days.

"A few years old?"

"I think so. It was taken somewhere in the Tucson area; that's all I know."

"We don't do too much with kids' sports. Maybe the scholastic editor would know. Was it a school program?"

"I don't think so."

"We only cover the high schools. You can imagine—boys, girls, baseball, softball, football, volleyball, soccer, swimming, track, and tennis." He seemed vaguely oppressed by the tidal wave of youthful athletes.

"They look younger than high school?"

"Oh, definitely. Junior high. Upper elementary, even. You might try Linda Baines in features. She handles some of the school stuff."

I thanked him and was passed on to Ms. Baines. Cheerful, pudgy, and energetic, she had a camera slung around her neck, a reporter's notepad in one hand, and a cup of coffee in the other.

"You just caught me. I'm rushing off to the Desert Museum, over in the Mountain Park. Wonderful program—the Gifted Elementaries. Have you seen our Mountain Park yet? Really a treasure. I think they're to be working with the aquariums today. Not such good photo ops as the animals, but you never know."

"I wonder if you'd recognize any of these children?" I said.

She peered at them for a moment. "Not in the Gifted Elementaries. Not the Musical Horizons. Arts for Everyone? I'm not sure about this little fellow. There's an awfully good cellist . . ."

"You wouldn't recognize the team, would you?"

"Dust Devils? That's really the sports department, isn't it?"

"They only cover the high school teams."

"Yes, of course. Community organizations, then. Now for those, you want Ruth Wilson if it's the calendar. She's our summer intern from State. Or Jose Esteban if it's local politics."

"I think the program was run by a priest. It's affiliated with one of the Catholic churches."

"Religion! Why didn't you say? You want Lydia Isavoli. She previews the sermons, handles cult news, really a mixed bag, Lydia's beat. Lydia," she called across the newsroom, "Lydia," then waved.

Lydia Isavoli studied the photo intently through a pair of oversized rose-tinted glasses, then glanced at me. "Well," she said.

"Yes?"

"Father Herman is suddenly popular."

I tried to hide my alarm. "Father Herman?"

"Someone who'd worked with him at Our Lady's just called the other day."

"What a coincidence," I said.

"Not that I'm surprised. Father's done wonders. He's a really remarkable man."

"So I've been told. I'd like to get in touch with him."

"Could I ask why?"

I was tempted to prevarication but fought down the impulse. "I'm a private detective. One of my clients has rather foolishly decided to jump bail. I want to convince her not to make a bad situation worse." I opened my wallet and handed over my license.

Ms. Isavoli gave a quick satisfied smile. "We all feel a little protective of Father Herman," she said. "We expect great things from him."

I wasn't quite sure what to say to that.

"He runs a mission now down near Nogales. The hierarchy can't quite decide whether they approve or not."

"How far away is the mission?"

"About sixty miles down Route Nineteen. It's called Casa Nueva. You can't miss it; it's right on the outskirts of town."

Ms. Isavoli's confidence proved exaggerated. Nogales struck me as drab, hot, and dusty, and Father Herman's Casa Nueva was by no means universally renowned. I stopped for a snack at a large and noisy sandwich shop, full of busloads of Mexico-bound shoppers and day-trippers. My order was processed with all deliberate speed, and my happiness was complete when the counter stool next to mine was taken by an aging derelict bundled into an immense and odoriferous brown tweed coat. He ordered a coffee, which he doctored with liberal doses of salt and sugar before he began rolling a cigarette.

My lunch compromised by the coat of a thousand and one nights, I decided to make the best of things.

"Excuse me," I said. "I'm trying to find a Father Herman. He runs something called the Casa Nueva. Would you know where that is?"

He studied me through a pair of wet red-rimmed eyes. "Yeah," he said at last.

"Near here?"

"Two, three miles." He licked the seam of his cigarette, tamped it on the counter, and rummaged through his pockets for a match.

"On this road?"

"Naw."

I looked up at the menu board for inspiration. The Shopper's Special, a double cheeseburger with fries and salad, seemed the best bet. "Care for a Shopper's Special?" I asked.

He took this under advisement. "Bacon and eggs is better."

I signaled one of the harried waitresses and gave the order.

"With hash browns," my companion added.

"With hash browns," I said. "Put it on my check."

There was a long silence until the plate came. My informant sampled the bacon, the eggs, and the hash browns in rotation, doused everything with catsup, relighted his cigarette, and proceeded to give me what proved to be succinct and accurate directions to Casa Nueva, a low white adobe building in a neighborhood of small houses, little gardens, and neglected yards.

Behind Casa Nueva lay open fields with a half-size soccer pitch, a small diamond, and a playground full of noisy little children. In front of the building, a signboard listed the hours for visiting-nurse appointments and a variety of community-group meetings and adult literacy classes, one of which was in progress inside.

I followed a hall decorated with children's artwork out to the playground. The supervisor was a pretty young woman with a lot of light brown hair and a great fund of patience and energy. She wore a ragged pair of jeans and a bright red Casa Nueva T-shirt, and when she saw me at the fence, she gave me a big smile and waved.

"I'm looking for Father Herman," I called. "Is he around?"

She looked at her watch. "He gets here around four."

"Could you tell me where I can find him?"

"He's at prayers at the moment," she said in a solemn voice. "He's never disturbed until four."

The ultimate "in conference." I returned to Nogales and found a motel room that featured, just as the manager had promised me, a fine view of the drab and uninspiring countryside. I phoned Harry, describing the town's monotonous scenery and tranquil air to assure him that everything was fine. He was not completely deceived and reported that the cops had been back and were peeved by my absence. I said that the trip was a piece of cake and Nogales one of the safest towns in the lower forty-eight. Nonetheless, I promised to be careful.

Next, I called the office, where I discovered that everything was definitely not fine.

"Envelope?" Martha asked.

"A medium-sized manila envelope with a note and a photo."

"There was nothing in the out basket when I came in this morning."

"Tell Garrett that he's to give you a copy—he'll know which photo—and that all his information is to be turned over to the police. Then fire him."

"You don't mean that," said Martha.

"I may very well mean it. Better yet, have him call me here. Tell him I'm not paying him for a single minute more on the Skane business. Nor Skipper, either."

Martha made soothing noises until I told her off, too, and slammed down the phone. I was feeling jumpy and out of sorts, a sort of psychic hangover from urban violence. The dun panorama of the desert ought to have been soothing but wasn't, and as soon as it got near four o'clock, I headed for the Casa Nueva.

This time, I stuck my head into one of the classrooms and asked after the good Father. I was directed to a tiny office, which proved empty, the screen exterior door ajar. Standing on the packed whitish dust outside, a man was studying the scrubby fields that ran from the Casa and the line of neighborhood houses to the bare purple hills in the distance. He was wearing jeans, boots, a Stetson hat, and a short-sleeved black shirt with a clerical collar.

"Father Herman?" I asked.

The priest was thin and tanned; straggling dark hair and a ragged beard framed an irregular bony face and brilliant light eyes. He looked like a second-string conquistador, but his melodious voice was soft and his manner gentle.

"You were looking for me earlier," he said.

"That's right. Anna Peters. I flew in yesterday from Washington."

"Washington State?"

"No, D.C."

"We don't often get visitors from so far away."

"I'm disappointed to hear that. I'd hoped I was your third D.C. visitor."

He gave me a quizzical look.

"Your old volunteer, Tony Skane," I said. "He disappeared with a woman named Maria Rivas. I believe he flew from Washington to Phoenix. My guess is that he came to see you."

Father Herman remained silent.

"Maria is out on bail, so she should not have left the District. That is the first problem. The second problem is that someone wants to kill her, which was probably why her bond was paid in the first place."

"What have you to do with the case?"

"Tony Skane hired me to investigate for the defense."

"But you were not successful?"

"I was partially successful. Just about the time our inquiries became promising, Maria's bail was mysteriously paid. But I trust you know all this. You do know where Tony and Maria are, don't you?"

"Yes," he said.

"It is absolutely vital that I talk to them. They are in serious danger."

"The reason they came west," Father Herman said.

"They're not going to be able to hide for very long. I found them in two days. And believe me, the competition is even more motivated."

Father Herman smiled. "You haven't found them yet," he said.

"The day before yesterday, I was nearly peppered with slugs from a thirty-eight Magnum. Fortunately, none of them hit me. Last week, one of Maria's coworkers at the Skanes' wasn't so lucky. She was deliberately run down and killed in Connecticut."

Father Herman's smile faded and he shook his head sadly.

"These are not nice people. In fact, after the other day, I'd say they are crazy people, definitely not amenable to reason, common sense, or appeals to their better nature."

"I hadn't any hopes along those lines."

"I'm glad to hear that, although I'm not sure it's consistent with your calling."

"My calling sometimes requires a good deal of flexibility."

"The point is, Tony and Maria need police protection and they need to return to Washington. If they do that, I'm hopeful we can clear Maria."

"I'm not at liberty to tell you where they are."

"Perhaps, then, you'd take a message to them. Tony knows who I am. Tell him there's more he doesn't know and that I need to see him as soon as possible."

"All right," said Father Herman. "But you must not try to follow me."

"Fair enough," I said, though I'd had that in mind until I thought about the open and deserted country. "But today. I can't stress the time factor enough."

"As soon as possible," he said. "And where will you be?"

"I'll be at my motel," I said, and gave him the name and the room number.

"I'll call you after nine tonight," Father Herman promised.

IN NOGALES, I had an excellent steak with baked beans on the side, a cowboy combination that I found eccentric. I was back in my room at 8:30, and Father Herman called at 9:05 with his regrets that neither Tony nor Maria was willing to see me.

"I can't believe that. Did you explain the situation to them?

"I did my best."

"Are they planning to hide here forever? I figure another day maximum before someone else makes the same connections I have. I can't tell you how lethal the opposition is."

"I advised them," Father Herman said. "I can't do anything more."

"If I could meet them somewhere—neutral ground. That way, there'd be no harm done if they didn't want to go back."

It was impossible, Father Herman said, and though he sounded worried, nothing I suggested could change his mind. I rehearsed all my arguments again while he murmured that it was impossible, that their minds were made up, that there was nothing to be done. Finally, I said I would stay another day for sure and asked him to call me again. He agreed to this and I put down the receiver.

I had visited Casa Nueva at just after four and Father Herman had called me at just after nine. Five hours. What did that suggest? Tony and Maria were a long way away and he had driven to see them? Tony and Maria were nearby and he had waited until after dark? Tony and Maria were entirely out of reach and had been called at a prearranged time?

I spread out the Arizona road map with its spider-web of red and gray roads and widely spaced tiny towns. Everywhere but Tucson and Phoenix looked like the back of beyond, and with the proximity to the border, Tony and Maria could already be in Mexico or heading west to L.A. or San Diego. At the end of an unrewarding hour, I had to conclude that my best hope was still Father Herman.

I THOUGHT IT WAS a branch of the magnolia at home scraping against the window, next, that the air conditioner had developed a tic or that Harry's quiet night breathing had stopped. Then I was awake. The heavy motel curtain shut out all but a sliver of the glaring orange floodlights; a truck down on the highway slowed into town and someone was tapping on the door of my room, softly but insistently.

I got out of bed, pulled on a pair of slacks, and drew the curtain back just a fraction. A stocky man, Mexican or Native American given his dark face and straight black hair, was standing by the door.

"Who is it?"

"From Father Herman," he whispered. "You must come quickly."

I took another look at his well-worn jeans, boots, and Stetson and slipped the bolt before I could think too much about it. "Come in. I'll be ready in a minute."

He stepped inside. "No lights," he said.

I grabbed a shirt, found my shoes, and stepped into the bathroom to dress. The fluorescent tubes turned the night to dazzling greenish yellow. It was 1:30. I switched off the light, opened the door, and fumbled in the dark for my wallet and my windbreaker. My small binoculars were still stuck in the pocket.

"Hurry," the man said. He moved softly over the rug and eased open the door to the second-floor veranda. He looked up and down, then gestured for me to follow. We walked quickly along the brightly lighted facade of the motel and down the outside stair into the shadows of the coarse shrubbery. When we were sure the parking lot was quiet, we ran across the asphalt to an old black truck.

"What's happened?" I asked when we were clear of the parking area and speeding along through the deserted streets of Nogales.

He gave a noncommittal grunt: classified information. His face was impassive, vaguely sinister. I hoped I had not underestimated the Colonel's subtlety—or his local contacts.

We drove for several miles in a generally westerly direction on a state road before turning off onto a dark, narrow, and unimproved secondary that petered out to a gravel track. My confidence in the whole venture was not increased when the driver switched off his headlights and drove with nothing but the parking lights. I've never been fond of mysterious midnight drives; this one was beginning to make me nervous.

I slipped my hand into my jacket pocket and curled my fingers around my miniature binoculars. Then we jounced down a slope that challenged all the ancient vehicle's springs, splashed through a trickle of water, and lurched up a slithery mess of stones and gravel to reach what was recognizably a road a few hundred yards away. I decided not to do anything precipitous until I was sure of finding my way back to civilization.

My companion began looking back into his mirror. "Hard for strangers," he said at last, with every sign of satisfaction, and put his foot on the gas. A few minutes later, I saw the faint glow of Nogales to my right; we had made a big rural circle and were heading due east. A quarter of an hour later, we pulled up behind Casa Nueva. My driver left the motor running and climbed down. "Wait here," he said.

A moment later, a thin man stepped from the back of the Casa, murmured thanks to the driver, and climbed into the cab. I was more relieved than I would have admitted to see Father Herman.

"What's happened?" I asked.

"I didn't really believe you," he said.

"There's been trouble."

"Two men came to the Casa this evening. One of our workers was shot."

"I'm sorry. Was it..."

"No, not fatal, by God's blessing. They asked for me, didn't believe I was not there, pulled handguns, and searched the place. Juan tried to get away and was shot. Fortunately, the neighbors came running, and the gunmen drove off."

"You've called the police?"

"They believe a robbery attempt—or an attempt at intimidation. We do a lot of work with migrant workers here."

"How likely is it?"

"Not very. My schedule is well known. Any local would know how to find me."

"Better change your routine," I said. "They'll surely try again."

"Who are these people?"

"My best guess is that they are money launderers, a rogue group not part of any of the big drug cartels. They joined up with a D.C. developer and restaurateur who needed cash. The expansion of his restaurant chain provided an old-fashioned but effective way to put illicit cash into legitimate circulation."

"Then his wife was murdered."

"Yes, not long after Maria had recognized one of the men involved. But so long as she was blamed for the fire, she was in no danger, especially while she was obviously suffering from shock. When I began looking into the case and made the connection between Skane and his criminal associates, the situation changed and she was suddenly released on bail."

"I understand," Father Herman said.

"What we still don't know is who actually set the fire. From the point of view of the case against Maria, that's the crucial question. I think she knows and her psychosomatic muteness comes from the fact that she's afraid to tell."

"She may still be afraid," Father Herman said.

"Agreed, but she's got less and less to lose."

There was little traffic on the road and we traveled fast for nearly ten miles before Father Herman turned off into a field. He dimmed his lights and we bumped along a farm track in semidarkness.

"Where are we?"

"Nearly there. A few years ago, some of us thought of establishing a retreat in this area."

There was not a light anywhere. "Seems like an ideal place," I said.

"It's beautiful, especially after the rains. This is where they filmed *Oklahoma*. It's all rolling grazing land, quite different from the desert immediately around Nogales."

"I'm not partial to the desert," I admitted.

"We bought an old ranch," he said.

He sounded wistful, and I asked, "But it didn't work out?"

"I decided we'd retreated too far already." He gave a rueful smile. "Nogales brings one up closer to the line, so to speak."

"Yes, I can see that."

"We sold the land to a conservation group, but we retained the actual ranch building. It's been years since we've done anything with it."

The truck jounced onto an even narrower and rougher track and he pointed ahead. There was a dark mass of trees against the night sky. As we came to a halt, I could just make out the rectangular shape of an old adobe building.

THIRTEEN

FATHER HERMAN shut off the motor and we listened to the long rustling grass and to the pings and sighs of the cooling engine. The truck doors sounded very loud when we got out. We stood for a moment in the field, in complete darkness except for a sprinkling of distant stars.

He went over and tapped twice on the plain, solid door. "It's Father Herman," he called softly.

The little adobe building looked deserted, but I heard Tony Skane whisper, "Who's with you?"

"Anna Peters, your investigator."

The old hinges creaked and a thread of light appeared. "I told you," Tony began, "that we didn't—"

"You've been followed already," the priest said. "There's been trouble at the Casa."

The light went out. We stepped inside and Tony bolted the heavy door behind us.

"Just a minute." He switched on his flashlight, revealing a plain square room with a brown tile floor, an old painted table, and a half dozen wooden chairs. Looking very young and determined, Tony relighted the kerosene lamp that was sitting on the table, hung it up on a dangling hook, and retrieved a .22 from where it had been resting against the doorjamb.

"What happened?"

"Two men came looking for you. There was a shooting. Juan Herrera will lose an eye."

"This is your fault," Tony said to me. "You followed us and led them to the Casa."

"Perhaps. More likely they made the same deductions I did."

"You could not have stayed here permanently, anyway," Father Herman said. "I think you should listen to what Anna has to say."

"We don't have much choice now."

"Where is Maria?" I asked.

"She's asleep," Tony said. "She needs to rest."

"It is her decision as well," I said, and took a step toward the back room.

"No," said Tony, but just then the rear door opened and Maria came into the room. She nodded to Father Herman and took Tony's arm. He spoke rapidly to her in Spanish, but though her eyes darkened, she did not lose her considerable self-possession. She turned to Father Herman and touched his arm sympathetically, then drew up one of the chairs and sat down, placing her hands on the table just the way she had in the interrogation room. I had a small pad of paper that I set in front of her and Father Herman produced a pen.

Maria hesitated, then picked up the pen and looked at me.

"I believe we can clear you," I said. "I believe that we can find out who set the fire. If so, you will be able to stay in this country if you wish and not have to remain in hiding."

As Tony started to translate this, she held up her hand and nodded to me to show that she understood.

"When I summarize what we have discovered, you will see that we can raise serious doubts about the charges. Enough, I believe, so that a jury would have reasonable doubt." I looked at Tony. "You should be pleased. Your money was well spent."

He looked more worried than happy.

"Nonetheless," I continued, "we have not been able to determine the crucial question; namely, who actually set the fire. That is what I need to ask you about."

"I know nothing about the fire," Maria wrote.

"That is not true," I said. "And I don't think you will swear to that with Father Herman as witness."

Maria fiddled nervously with the pen.

"You have been protecting someone."

Maria said nothing.

"And you haven't been completely candid. Your trips, for one thing. Any prosecutor would want to know how you put so much mileage on your *moto*."

Maria scribbled a line. "'That has nothing to do with the case,'" Tony translated. "That's true," he added.

"You know where she was going?"

Maria made a peremptory gesture, and Tony looked unhappy. "She visited her grandmother."

"Her grandmother? What was the big secret?"

"Nothing. Some problem with her visa."

I foresaw trouble with Immigration, but that was irrelevant at the moment. "So, there was no mysterious contact. That suggests you were protecting someone closer to home. Was it Tony?''

"Just a minute," he exclaimed, and Maria shook her head vigorously.

"I think you are lying. You are protecting Tony, not because he set the fire or had anything to do with it but because you have a good idea who did. And every good possibility comes back to Joe Skane or to his associate, Colonel Garcia, or to one of their employees. That's right, isn't it?''

Maria buried her face in her hands, and Tony jumped up and put his arm around her. "She's been under a terrible strain," he said.

"The strain of lying," I said. "The strain of being a suspect. You must decide whether to face the truth and clear Maria or to preserve your ignorance and force her into hiding."

Maria shook her head and reached for Tony's hand.

"The truth can clear her, and if we make it public, it can protect both of you and Luisa Ceasario, too. But we need a statement and we need to get you back to Washington as soon as possible."

Tony drew his hand away from Maria and stood up very straight. "She is afraid my father is the one."

Maria shook her head and caught at his arm.

"That's why she's refused to speak and why she refused to see me. It's true," he said, looking at her sadly. "She blames herself because she told Mother about the colonel. Maria was terrified when she saw him; she was ready to leave and Mother got it out of her. That was the last straw, wasn't it?''

"I'm not quite sure I understand," I said.

"Mother told my father he would have to get rid of the colonel—and his profitable connections. That's when he asked her for money again."

"So that he wouldn't have to be dependent on the colonel's cash?"

"Yes, something like that. I'm not sure why she wouldn't give him the cash. Perhaps because of Natalie Welsung; perhaps just because she was sick and tired. I don't know. She wasn't always very reasonable the last year or so."

"And so your father arranged the fire to prevent the exposure of his criminal connections and to make himself independent again with your mother's money."

"I'm sure of it," Tony said. "I was afraid of it right from the start, but there was no evidence, and we were all at the party. He couldn't possibly have set the fire himself, if the times are right."

"Maria knows something more," I said.

She shook her head.

"You said you fell asleep in your room and woke up with the smell of smoke in the dark. Yet normally, if you were at home alone with Mrs. Skane, you stayed downstairs in the atrium."

Maria stayed immobile.

"You must tell her," Tony said after a minute. "I know the worst already."

She looked at him, doubtful and anxious, and he sat down beside her and put the pen in her hand. After a long moment, she began to write in Spanish. "'Everyone was to go out that evening except John and me.

While I was fixing the señora's dinner tray, Señor Skane came into the pantry with a bottle of champagne. He poured a glass for her and insisted I keep the bottle.' "

"Was that unusual?"

" 'Very. He was generous with liquor, but this was fine French champagne. He seemed in a happy mood.' "

"And Mrs. Skane? What sort of mood was she in?"

" 'She was fine, quite cheerful, in fact. After dinner, I went to sit downstairs in the atrium as I usually did, and I read until nine, when I checked on Señora Skane again. She said she was just going to sleep. I went back downstairs and made a cup of coffee and sat down to drink it before I went upstairs.' "

"So you *were* sitting in the atrium?"

She nodded and sat motionless, as if reluctant to proceed, then began in the rapid jagged script that signaled deep emotional distress. "I heard a golf motor.' "

"A golf motor?" I asked Tony.

"I think she means a golf cart," Tony said, and Maria nodded.

"What time was this?"

" 'Maybe nine-twenty, maybe later.' "

"Ask her where it was coming from," I told Tony.

" 'It was coming from the back of the property. I was upset, because I knew it would be Señor Skane. He had been giving me trouble since the party.' "

"Ever since he knew you had recognized the colonel?"

"'Yes. Señora Skane had told him. At first, he hadn't seemed worried. In fact, he made a joke of it. Then later, although he knew I was frightened, he said he'd tell the colonel that he'd been recognized, that he was famous.'"

"And later?"

"'Later, when there was trouble with the señora, he kept after me to say I'd been mistaken, that the colonel wasn't the man I'd thought.'"

"What did you do when you heard the cart?"

"'I went upstairs right away.'"

"So you didn't actually see who it was?"

She shook her head. "'No, but I had no doubt. The señor was the only one who regularly used the golf cart.'"

Of course, I thought, she had not seen the video of the fund-raiser; she had no way of knowing that Joe Skane had an airtight alibi.

"'He went into the atrium, I think, by the side entrance.'"

"That's the entrance by the pool and the entertainment area?"

"'Yes, because I looked out the back windows and couldn't see anyone.'"

"Did you go downstairs?"

She shook her head.

"What did you do?"

"'I phoned Luisa and Antonia. They were at a party in D.C.'"

"To tell them?"

"'No, just to talk to them. I did not want to know that Señor Skane was in the house. I locked my door, turned out the lights, and called the party. I had promised I would call. We knew the people; it was a *quinceanera* party for a friend's daughter.'" She looked at Tony.

"Sort of a debut, a coming-out party for a fifteen-year-old. The traditional age," he said.

"This was never mentioned," I said. The Ceasarios had testified that they'd gone to a movie.

"'They did not want to involve our friends,'" Tony translated.

"Illegals?"

She shrugged, then wrote on the pad. "'I am not sure. Anyway, it seemed safer to say that I had been asleep. I did not want to be involved. I did not want to know.'"

"And what exactly did you tell Antonia and Luisa?"

"'I mentioned that Señor Skane had returned home.'" She looked embarrassed. "'It was sort of a joke. We didn't take the señor too seriously, but we all kept out of his way.'"

"So they knew the approximate time the person who set the fire had arrived at the house."

"'Yes.'"

"Anything else?"

"'I think I mentioned the golf cart, that he'd come by golf cart. We were not taking it seriously. I mean, they were not and I was trying not to. I said he'd given the señora and me champagne and they were teasing me about that. Then I talked briefly to some of our friends and said good night.' "

"And then?"

" 'I went to the window and looked out and listened for the golf cart.' "

"Did you hear anything?"

She shook her head. " 'I wanted to know if he had gone. I went down the stairs at the side....' "

"Not the stair to the atrium in the center of the building?"

" 'No, the stair at the other end of the hallway. It leads out to the side of the building and to the entertainment complex.' "

"Go on."

" 'I walked past the swimming pool and the changing room.' " She stopped writing, as if puzzled. " 'There was an unfamiliar smell.' "

"An unfamiliar smell?"

" 'Not cleaning liquid or chlorine or even the señor's aftershave lotion.' "

"What did it smell like?"

She thought a minute. " 'It smelled like gardenias. It smelled like the gardenias Andrew brought in for the señora during the winter.' "

"A perfume perhaps?"

She nodded. " 'A perfume like gardenias. I had forgotten that.' "

I had to contain my exasperation. Maria's fears and assumptions and her edited testimony had cost her several months in jail, put both her and Tony in danger, and perhaps sealed Antonia Ceasario's fate. Save us from good intentions! "Go on," I said.

"'Then as soon as I opened the door to the hall leading to the atrium, I smelled the smoke and felt the heat.'"

"Were the lights still on?"

"'The lights had been on in the pool area, but when I approached the atrium, everything went dark and then the fire just exploded.'"

Maria's description of the fire in her original statement had been convincing because it was true; she had simply transposed her location.

"Did you ever get upstairs again?"

"'Yes, but I couldn't get into the atrium; the flames were terrible. I got back through the sports complex and went up the outer stair, but I couldn't reach my room.'"

"So you went back down and out to the lawn, where John Delano saw you."

She nodded. "'He asked me if the señora was safe. I tried to tell him that she was trapped inside, but when I opened my mouth, nothing came out.'"

"There is only one more thing. Did you have any other chance to communicate with the Ceasarios?"

She shook her head, "'The medics took me to the hospital that night for shock. Luisa and Antonia left two days later, I believe.'"

"That's right," Tony said. "The police questioned them and Dad gave them notice as soon as they were finished."

"They said nothing about the phone call, the party, nothing," I said.

"They were afraid of harming their friends," Tony said. "They would never volunteer anything."

"They didn't say anything? Not even to you?" I asked Tony.

"Especially not to me. They did not want to be involved and they did not want to involve my family."

I must have looked doubtful, because Tony added, "Besides, they would have been afraid of the colonel. Whether they knew him or not, they knew his type. They didn't want anything to do with military men from home."

"Yet if our assumptions are correct, the colonel was only concerned with continuing his convenient relationship with Skane Enterprises. He had a vested interest in keeping your mother alive and in control of her own money."

"Yes," Tony said bitterly, "but someone else did not."

FOURTEEN

"WE HAVE TO GET YOU out of here," I said after Father Herman and I had signed Maria's statement.

"I think we might be safer in daylight," Father Herman said. "At this time of night, any traffic is pretty obvious."

There was certainly something to that. "Where's the nearest phone?"

"Center of Patagonia. But it's inside the general store."

"That's no problem," I said. "But you're right; we don't want to attract unnecessary attention."

"It's nearly three," Tony said. "We can get a couple of hours' rest and leave at sunrise."

We discussed this but could not come up with anything better. Maria and Tony both looked exhausted and went to try to sleep. Father Herman and I sat in the dark with one of the shutters open and took turns checking outside the house for anything that sounded suspicious. Father Herman had a pipe that he prepared and smoked with ceremonious deliberation. It gave him an air of calm unconcern that I found myself unable to share.

Beyond our silence was a good deal of unfamiliar noise: the wind sweeping the grass, the sounds of strange insects, and, in the distance, coyotes and a bird, which the good father told me was a small owl.

"Are you from this area?" I asked.

"L.A. originally. I wanted something different."

"Like Tony Skane."

"I think Tony will settle for romance."

"His late mother would have been relieved. She was apparently afraid he'd become a monk or study for the priesthood."

"I thought he might, too. He wanted to escape from things, from the things of the material world."

"You'd understand that if you saw his home and met his father."

"Maybe this is better for him," Father Herman said reflectively. "You can escape too far and then you have to come back."

"To Nogales?" I suggested.

"To Nogales," he agreed, "whereas Tony..."

"This should be enough romance to last him."

"It would certainly be enough for me," the priest said.

"You're like me. You're outgrowing the taste for these excitements."

He smoked in silence for a time. I got up and listened at the door a moment, then walked around the back of the building. The dry fields were rustling like a grass skirt, and though the stars were still very bright in the clear sky, the east was beginning to turn a pale soft gray. I walked just beyond the truck, but there was no sound except the wind and the grass and my own footsteps. I was about to return when I heard a car. It sounded quite far away—on the main road, I was sure. But on closer acquaintance, there was something irregular about the engine, as if it was struggling up a rough track.

I ran back into the house. "I hear a car," I said, but Father Herman was already calling Tony and Maria. Tony grabbed the rifle and we scrambled out to the truck.

Outside, everything was quiet again. "I don't hear anything," he said.

We listened: the wind, the grass, a bird, nothing else.

"Anyone from the Casa would drive right up," Father Herman said.

"I could have been mistaken. It could have been out on the main road."

Father Herman shook his head.

"They'll know we're here right away when they hear the truck," Tony said.

"They might be walking up the track. Is there a way out through the fields?"

"Yes," Father Herman said, "but then we'd better head back to Nogales instead of trying to reach Tucson."

"We'd better do that, anyway," I said. "This truck won't keep ahead of them for long."

Tony climbed in the back of the pickup with the rifle as Father Herman, Maria, and I squeezed into the front seat. The click of the doors sounded very loud in the quiet dawn; the engine turned over with a deafening roar before it coughed and died.

"It's cold," Father Herman said apologetically.

He turned the key again; the engine rumbled ineffectually but refused to budge. He fiddled with the choke. Tony leaned out of the back and said, "I hear a car starting up."

I looked out the truck window. The house was solid but hardly defensible with a single rifle; the fields were completely open; dawn was coming. Our chances did not look good.

Father Herman sat motionless for a moment, then adjusted the choke, turned the key, and pumped the accelerator; the ancient machine growled and wheezed, roared, stuttered, faded, then caught. "We'll have to give it a minute," he said. "It's temperamental."

I saw pinpoints of light over the fields. "Don't give it too long; they're on their way," I said.

When he let out the clutch, the truck reluctantly bounced forward. We swung around the corner of the house, almost stalled by a half-collapsed barn, and went through an old wire fence into a field. From there on, Father Herman drove without lights and with surprising élan. We cruised along a row of fencing and rolled down into a ditch so steep that Maria and I clutched the dashboard. Father Herman flicked on the headlights for an instant, revealing a bank a good ten feet high on the opposite side.

"Washout," he said, braking suddenly and spinning the wheels sharply to the right. Tony let out a yell in the back and we heard him slide against the cab. I thought we'd be stuck for sure, but if temperamental, the ancient truck was also high and solid on its axles. We raced down the dry streambed, jouncing over rocks and sliding on the loose gravel. Twice we had to stop to move branches, but at last the high sides of our miniature canyon subsided and, yelling, "Hang on," Father Herman steered the truck back up a grade into the fields.

"I don't see them," Tony called, and Father Herman gave the thumbs-up sign before endangering the undercarriage in a top-speed rush that ended when we skidded onto a farm track.

"This takes us out to the state road," he said. A half mile farther, we met an unlocked steel gate. Beyond was a narrow paved road, and we set out at good speed toward Nogales. We had just passed the cluster of homes and stores of Patagonia when a car without lights shot out from behind a curve and pulled in front of the truck.

The brakes gave a terrible shriek. Father Herman wrenched the wheel and the truck veered into the oncoming lane before its back end slewed around and caught the side of the car with a shuddering crash. We were all stunned for a moment, then I saw someone move in the car. "Start the engine," I yelled to Father Herman.

"They may be hurt. I'll just see—"

"Better for us if they are hurt. We've got to get out of here."

He was set to protest when a shot whanged off the top of the truck and sent further shivers down the cracked windshield. The truck's engine began coughing ineffectually. I opened the door, grabbed Maria's arm, and slid out, pulling her after me. Someone shouted and there was a shot as we stumbled into the grass and shrubbery at the side of a field. "Come on; come on. They can't follow all of us," I said when she hung back. "Tony'll get out the back of the truck."

It was still fairly dark, especially against the glaring lights from the two vehicles stranded on the road. The several shots that followed us whistled harmlessly overhead. We hit a wire fence and scrambled under the lowest strands as the dawn was split by the roar and whoosh of an explosive fire. Maria froze in terror, half-crouched by the fence. "It's our best chance," I said. I grabbed her arm again and started to run.

Well out of sight of the main road, we crossed a sandy track and I stopped, my lungs on fire and my leg muscles disengaged. "I'm not as young as I used to be," I told Maria.

She looked back toward the road.

"We have to hope Tony and Father Herman got away on the other side," I said. "It'll do them no good for us to be caught here."

Although she didn't seem convinced, she pointed down the path. The sky was definitely gray now. We hurried toward the only cover around, a surprisingly well-wooded area with thick coverts of shrubbery. Half the birds of Arizona were congregated in the branches; underneath their chirping and calling was the sound of running water. A few yards farther along, Maria touched my shoulder and pointed to a sign. We were in a wildlife refuge.

"That's us," I said, "wildlife in need of refuge. Maybe there'll be a park ranger or a nature center with a telephone."

She stopped again. I could tell she wanted to go back to the road.

"We can't risk it," I said. "If they get you, they'll kill us all. Without you, they may spare Tony and Father Herman in the hope of finding you."

I wasn't sure how logical that was, but it was the best I could do on two hours of sleep and no breakfast. Although Maria looked skeptical, she followed me into the reserve, which was laid out along a shallow, meandering stream. The waterway wasn't much by eastern standards, but clearly every drop was precious in a dry land. Immense heavy-limbed cottonwoods grew nearest the water; a little farther out were thickets of bushy shrubs, broken here and there by clearings full of long buff and amber grasses. According to the reserve map that was pinned to a large rustic signboard, the whole made a lazy circuit about half a mile in diameter. "No sign of any buildings," I said.

So far as I could tell from the reserve map, we were somewhere to the west of the town. I traced the line with my finger. "This direction," I said. "But I think it's going to be too light now to walk safely."

Maria nodded.

"We'd better see if there's some help around. If not, we can hide here all day."

We walked the length of the reserve trail, finding neither ranger nor phone, and at last we settled on an open grassy patch behind a thick screen of trees. Maria checked the ground with elaborate care for snakes. I was too tired to bother. I sat down on a likely patch of turf and leaned against the truck of a small tree.

AROUND MY HEAD, a fly buzzed and the harsh-voiced bird that had been rustling and scolding in the branches fell silent. I realized that I had been asleep for some time. My back was stiff, the sun had lost its red dawn tinge, and two people were approaching slowly and carefully along the reserve trail.

I moved my legs cautiously and lifted my head. Through the leaves, I saw a dark shirt and khaki slacks that raised hopes of a reserve warden. Then I saw a stubby handgun and held my breath. A soft murmur came from the searchers; I could see the second now, a stout dark man in jeans and sunglasses.

Maria turned slightly in her sleep and I touched her shoulder to warn her. When she opened her eyes, I put my finger to my lips and nodded toward the path. "They can't see us," I whispered.

She gave me a quizzical look. I remembered the pale powdery sand of the paths and tapped my foot.

The two men had turned around; it sounded as if they were pushing through the brush above the stream. Maria and I got to our feet, crossed the little clearing, and edged into the thicket beyond. Almost immediately we heard the crackle of branches and dropped down again. They had regained the trail and, swearing softly at the heat and vegetation, were starting in our direction.

All I could see through the leaves were one man's shoes: black loafers, whitened with the dry earth of the trail. The shoes stopped, and I realized that the men had lost our footprints on the grassy reserve path. They were moving slowly, checking both sides, and though they seemed more interested in the stream side at the moment, sooner or later they would poke into the little thicket where Maria and I were hiding.

I looked over my shoulder to check our line of retreat. Behind us was a fallen tree, a tangle of branches, and what appeared to be another narrow path. If the two gunmen turned onto it, they could not help seeing us. Maria had noticed the same thing, because she gripped my arm. I nodded, but there was nowhere we could go without alerting them.

The men began walking toward us again and we ducked our heads and held our breath. Sweat began running down my face and dropping like rain onto the dusty grass.

"Look out," someone said. They were so close now that I could see that the man had torn one cuff, that his slacks were rumpled, and that he was wearing a large and expensive gold watch.

"What?" the other one asked.

"Excellent habitat for spring warblers," a high, well-projected woman's voice said, "but at this season we can hope for hawks, the rose-throated becard, and..."

There was an appreciative murmur.

"Not so good as up in the Huachuca Mountains, but we have the broad-billed here, and on a good day..."

"Shit," said the guy with the black shoes under his breath. He stuck the handgun into the belt of his pants.

"What the hell are they doing here?" his companion growled.

"You saw the sign. It's a reserve for birds. They've come to see them."

"Morning," the woman called cheerfully. "Wonderful day."

Black Shoes allowed that it was.

"Have you gone up to the north trail yet?"

"Naw. We only had a little time," he said.

"A shame to miss it; it's our open savanna. The best habitat for hawks and finches. And I forgot to mention the five-striped sparrow."

At the idea of seeing this rarity, the group of birders rose like hounds on a scent.

"Not every day, of course," their guide assured them, "but we have hopes. Tom saw one yesterday. You're welcome to join us."

"We've got to be going, but thanks."

"Come again," the guide said pleasantly. "Ah, now what's that?"

With a rustle, all the birders raised their field glasses.

"Sounds like a cardinal," someone said.

"You're close; that's what it would be in the East, but it's a shorter song. There's his other call. That's the Pyrrhuloxia."

"There he is."

"Where?"

"More to the right."

"Oh yes, that's him."

I stood up as quietly as I could and motioned for Maria. As soon as the birders had digested the Pyrrhuloxia and moved along the trail, Maria and I slid through the brush and reached the side path.

"We'll join them," I said. I still had my jacket with me and in it my small binoculars. "We'll get you in their bus or whatever."

Maria looked dubious.

"You've hurt your ankle. We got a ride out from town. I'll think of something. Limp on command and carry these." I handed her the binoculars. "No, this way," I said, showing her the adjustment. "Just smile and look knowledgeable."

We left our cover and hurried after the group. At the juncture of the trails, we stopped, but our pursuers were nowhere in sight. "They're probably waiting until this tour group goes," I said.

If so, they'd no doubt be lurking about the entrance. Though that made a difficulty with my plan, I didn't see any alternative. The amount of cover in the reserve was definitely finite, and, once away from the stream, the land was wide open.

I tried to remember the red trail diagram that had decorated the signboard; it was important to join the group early enough so that our approach to the parking lot would be protected, but not so early that we might be counseled to limp on ahead and wait by their transport. That would never do.

We moseyed along behind the group, passing our binoculars back and forth and focusing on whatever limb or bush the group was studying. Gradually, I struck up a conversation with an older couple in matching white porkpie hats. They were with a birding tour that was due to cross into Mexico as soon as they finished in the reserve.

"You'll cross at Nogales?"

"Yes, it's the nearest border crossing, then south to San Blas. Wonderful sea and water birds and the Singaita forest. We're hoping for nearly one hundred species."

"Good luck," I said. "I wonder if your van—"

"Bus," the woman said, "but it's not too big."

"A minibus," her husband said.

"I wonder if there would be a couple of extra seats. My friend turned her ankle and it's going to be a long wait for our ride."

"Well, you'll have to ask Judith, our guide. I'm not sure there's room with all the knapsacks and lunches...."

"People bring far too much stuff," her husband said. "Though there are racks for luggage."

"There," said his wife. "Up there. That's a gray hawk, I'm sure."

"Good eye! A gray hawk, everyone," the leader announced.

The group pivoted, binoculars up, and I nudged Maria, whispered, "Limp," and moved through the group toward Judith, who looked smart and practical.

"Never a good idea to rely too much on getting picked up," she said in response to our problem. "Tourists forget the heat here at midday." She looked permanently sun-cured.

"Heat all day as far as I'm concerned," I said, and elaborated on a story of promised rides and interlocking schedules that seemed less and less plausible the longer it ran.

"We're really crowded," she said doubtfully. "But maybe your friend could squeeze in. If you don't mind holding a couple of bags..."

Maria smiled and nodded. I pulled her arm over my shoulder and helped her along the final yards to the bus. Our feet crunched on the gravel; a bird scolded in the brush. Over my heartbeat, I kept listening for the sound of men pushing through the shrubs, for the sudden acceleration of a car, for the high, nasty whine of a bullet, but the sun-dappled cottonwoods, the dark thread of the stream, the shady parking lot with the minibus all seemed peaceful. If the two well-armed visitors and their vehicle were still around, they were well out of sight, and it struck me that violence is not so much an intrusion as a completely different world, a passage through the mirror obtained by folly, recklessness, or bad luck.

While Maria and I stood sweating with fear, the birding group, happy and oblivious, milled around with bottles of water and reserve checklists. As they prepared to leave, there was renewed discussion about seats, but the elderly couple we'd befriended offered to squeeze over, and at last Maria was helped onto the bus. I slipped her my room key, thanked the couple and Judith, and climbed back out.

The doors closed, the driver started the engine, and, almost subliminally, I heard another engine; safety had been an illusion after all. I gave a hasty wave and walked quickly back up the trail, hoping Maria wouldn't be spotted on the bus.

FIFTEEN

I STARTED TO RUN as soon as I was out of sight. A wild thought of crossing the reserve and picking my way downstream didn't last more than a hundred yards. I've never been much of an athlete and that, plus advancing age and Arizona heat, brought me to my senses pretty quickly: I needed somewhere to hide.

When I reached the reserve signboard, I stopped to catch my breath and noticed a narrow path that wound out of sight between some shrubs. I figured it couldn't provide any worse cover than what I'd already seen. Fifty yards along, I spotted a weathered shed under a group of cottonwoods. A burst of speed brought me to a row of boarded-up windows. A door at the side opened on a little bare room with benches around the edges: a birding blind.

I stepped back out. The meager space between the pilings seemed no safer than the open interior and promised snakes in addition. I seemed to have reached, quite literally, a dead end. I was wondering whether to dash back to the main trail or to set off through the brush when I heard someone coming.

Danger concentrates the mind wonderfully. The shed interior and substructure were useless as hiding places; the roof, shaded by cottonwoods and steeply sloped away from the path, suddenly became a possibility. I jerked open a window, set one foot on the sill, and hauled myself up.

I grabbed for the roof and felt the dry and crumbling edges of old wood shingles. That was bad. What was worse was that the roof was considerably higher than I had estimated. I tried to pull myself up, got halfway, and felt the edges of the shingles start to give. My arms trembling with the strain, I got ready to hit the ground.

A twig cracked somewhere behind me, and, newly inspired, I stepped up onto the hinged window cover. It swung back against the building and I heaved myself up. The window cover's hinges gave with a creak, but I got one leg onto the roof, scraping my knee and both hands in the process. As I hauled my other leg up, someone ran heavily down the path and stamped into the blind. I slid out of sight and flattened myself against the shingles.

He rustled around inside the blind for a moment, then I heard the sound of the door. From the way he kept walking back and forth, I could tell that he was suspicious, but like most people, he did not think of looking overhead. Meanwhile, I began to grill. Even through the tree branches, the sun was hot. I could feel my sweaty fingers beginning to slip on the steeply angled shingles.

After a few minutes, the man below stopped moving, and I eased my head up a fraction. The line of shrubs came into view. A little higher and I would be able to see the path, but I felt myself start to slip and clutched the roof again.

"Charlie?" the man below called softly.

"Yeah."

The colonel, too. Great!

I could hear him coming along the trail and waited for the fellow below to join him. Nothing. I risked stretching my neck. I could see the path curve and disappear under the mesh of overhanging branches. Nothing more.

"You see anything?"

"Naw."

Something told me the man below was uneasy. Could he see my shadow? Had he stepped far enough back to see the top of the roof? I raised my head and worked myself a couple of inches farther up the roof, but that was a mistake, because I put one knee on a shingle that tore free and precipitated me down the back of the blind. I grabbed for the peak of the shed's roof, missed, tried for the side, tore away another shingle, and slid uncontrollably down the steep surface, leaving chunks of my hands and legs as I went.

Down below, I heard an exclamation, a shot, and then one of the overhanging limbs cracked my back and slowed my descent enough so that I wound up dangling off the back of the blind. From the front came the sounds of a brief but violent struggle. I let go of the roof and dropped into a mess of thorns and branches.

Someone gave a cry; there was a blow, then the sound of a heavy body falling. I stuck my head around the side wall and saw Mike Garrett take a stout-looking revolver from its supine owner.

"It's me," I said. "Don't shoot."

Though he jumped a foot and came down with his pistol at the ready, he didn't. "Nice diversion," he said.

"Thanks." I tried futilely to brush the splinters out of my bleeding hands and realized that I was shivering despite the Arizona sun.

"Where's the colonel?"

"Up the other way. Unless he's deaf, he's sure to be along."

Mike stuck the extra revolver in his belt and grabbed the man by the collar. "Best put him in the shed."

We dragged my would-be assailant out of the way, tied him up with our belts, and sat down to wait in the stifling blind with all the windows closed. My legs began to get stiff, and my back was throbbing.

The minutes passed; Mike looked at his watch. "How big's this place?"

"There's a couple of miles of trail, no more. I just got to the blind. He can't be too far away."

Mike stood up and swore under his breath. "He'll have bugged out. That's the kind he is."

"I'm all for getting out of here myself," I said.

We eased out the door and along the path. There was no one in sight at the signboard and no one at the main entrance.

"Where's your car?" I asked.

"On a farm track I found up the way."

"Did you see their car?"

"Theirs? Yours, you mean."

I was surprised.

"Standard white Chevy rental. I'd gotten your plate number before I arrived."

"They must have stolen it from the motel lot last night."

"Be glad they did. I picked up the accident on my police scanner, got to the scene, and . . ."

I had already started to run—down the path, through the barway at the entrance, up the dusty access road. "Where was it?" I asked.

"Just up ahead. There's a little pull off. What's the hurry? He's gone for sure."

"Yes, and he has my car, which means he knows where I was staying. I gave Maria my room key. If he thinks to go there . . ."

Mike sprinted ahead, but the colonel either had not noticed the car tucked away behind some trees or had not wished to lose any time. The tires were intact and the engine started up without a murmur.

"We'll get him," Mike said, his face intent.

"Please remember, he's not our priority."

"We'll get him sure," he repeated.

On the dashboard was a half container of coffee, lukewarm and sticky-sweet. "I don't know why you put so much sugar in it," I complained. My hands felt as if they'd been flayed, and after being cold, I was now beginning to feel queasy in the heat.

"There's a doughnut, too," Mike said.

It was a half-melted cream-filled number that looked disgusting. I ate two-thirds of it and littered Arizona with the rest. Revived by the sugar, I checked my watch. "How far ahead do you think he'll be?"

"Ten minutes? I don't think we were in that shed more than five, ten minutes."

"Time for him to find the room."

"If she went there."

"Where else? She doesn't speak. She'd have shown them the room key. I told them the name of the motel."

In response, Mike floored the accelerator. We went racing down the dusty highway, whipping around laboring trucks, and cut through a gas station lot to avoid a school bus.

"Jesus! Mike!"

"We can't afford to miss him," he said.

"For our client's sake," I said.

His look told me I was wasting my breath; he was completely focused on the colonel.

"Understand we're not risking her life, not to mention our own, on some personal crusade."

"In Guatemala, he had protection. In Panama, he was untouchable," Mike said reflectively. "But you know, I was always confident he'd show up here. I've been on the alert for him for a dozen years. I just knew he'd come."

"Why would he have left Panama, where he was rich and protected?" I asked, interested in spite of myself. "It doesn't make sense."

"It doesn't make sense," Mike agreed. "The colonel doesn't make sense—not unless you have his mentality. He doesn't care about money. I'm not even sure he cares about power, except in specific instances. He likes killing; that's what he likes. And he likes doing it himself."

"Remember, we've got nearly enough to get him legally. No damage done. I'm sure he knows about the fire."

"Fire!" Mike exclaimed. "What was the fire? One rich old lady dead. He'd be out in twenty years." Mike's eyes were bright and furious. "She was eighteen, the girl he 'disappeared.' He's already had a dozen years too long."

"The motel's the next left," I warned as he stamped angrily on the gas. "Pull into the back and stop by the trash recycler."

We skidded to a stop and Mike asked, "Which floor?"

"Second. But we'll be less obvious if we go up this stairway and into the hall."

"One at each entrance," Mike advised. "He'll be on the alert."

"Let's be sure he's here first." I leaned over the veranda; the parking lot was filled with seemingly identical light-colored cars bearing rental-company plates.

Mike's eyes were sharper than mine. "There. Parking space three-ten."

"Right below my room."

He nodded. "I want the outside," he said. "He may make a break for the car."

I could tell that Mike was looking forward to the possibility, but there wasn't much I could do about that if I wanted to get Maria out. "Keep out of sight for a minute. Since he doesn't know what I look like, I may be able to talk my way inside."

Mike hesitated, then held up five fingers and started down the veranda. It was 10:00 a.m. Inside, the cleaners were bustling up and down with carts of linens while tourists packed for the day's trips. Decimated room-service breakfast trays left a lingering scent of eggs and bacon that mingled with the smells of cleaning powder and new carpet; a small boy was playing with a remarkably noisy windup toy in the open doorway of his room.

The colonel had been maybe ten minutes ahead of us. How long to find the right room? How long to persuade Maria to open the door or to force the lock? However I figured it, he'd still had too much time. We were late, maybe too late, and when I saw that a cleaner had left her keys stuck in one of the doors, I didn't hesitate.

I jerked the key out of the lock, grabbed the first linen cart I saw, and charged toward my room. I had almost reached the door when I heard a voice calling, "Miss! Señora!" with increasing volume and anxiety. I stuck the key in the door. It refused to turn, sending my heart into overdrive. I tried another key, felt it engage, and shouted, "Maid service!"

There was a sound from the room and a shout from the indignant chambermaid down the corridor. I caught a glimpse of a dark man in the narrow entryway of the room and sent the loaded cart into him with all my strength.

The discharge of the handgun deafened me. I thought, I've been shot; I'm dead on my feet. Then I saw that both man and gun were on the floor, struggling out from under the cart, sheets, towels, loose toilet rolls, and complimentary mints. I put one foot on his wrist and kicked the gun away with the other.

Someone with a supersonic flood of Spanish tugged at my arm. "Call the police," I shouted. *"¡Policía, pronto!"*

I think she'd have given me an argument if Mike had not chosen that moment to fire into the outside lock, smashing it noisily. The sound also inspired the colonel, who grabbed one of my ankles and tipped me onto the floor. I threw a heap of towels over his head, but he flailed around, got to his knees, and made a dive for the pistol. Before I could even open my mouth, Mike had fired at point-blank range.

There was a scream from the corridor; a red plume rose and spread against the wall and the acrid smell of gunpowder and the raw meaty smell of blood filled the room. I pushed myself back from the mess encroaching on the pastel carpet and struggled to my feet with the help of the overturned cart.

Mike was standing perfectly still, his face immobile, his eyes expressionless. Well trained as ever, he bent down and picked up the discarded handgun, but he didn't need to examine the colonel. He turned to where Maria was cowering against the wall. *"Está muerto, señorita,"* he said, and gave a formal little bow.

She was silent for several seconds and then in a low, strange, unused voice, she said, *"Muchas gracias, señor."*

SIXTEEN

THE HOSPITAL ROOM was plush and comfortable, with tasteful wallpaper, framed prints, and a private bath. The big window gave a nice view of the setting sun and, underneath the casement, an efficient air conditioner took one's mind off the heat. This was my second trip. I'd already been down to the emergency room to get a tetanus shot and to have assorted surface abrasions cleaned and stitched. After that, I'd had a detour to the local police station, where I'd given a long statement and said with a straight face and nearly total conviction that Garrett had fired on the colonel in self-defense.

It had taken time to explain to the authorities, unhappy about gunfire at the normally tranquil La Perfecta Motel, why I had felt obliged to purloin a service cart and break into my own room. At one sticky point, I fortunately remembered the colonel's associate, who was removed from the birding blind suffering a nasty headache and the beginnings of heat exhaustion. His record came up in gaudy detail on the police computer, and though the late colonel's mouthpiece would huff and puff about his legitimate interests and patriotic services, there was no such mitigation possible for his colleague.

Finally, I'd had a session with a member of the local legal fraternity, a fellow complete with fluffy sideburns, a Stetson hat, red boots, and a pinstriped suit. Once this legal cowpoke had earned his fee, I was put in touch with Deirdre Silverbaum, Executive Security's own lawyer in D.C. I gave Deirdre a digest of the situation. When I finished, there was a long silence at the other end. I imagined her doing quick sums on her little calculator.

"And Mike Garrett? Does he have his own legal counsel?" she asked.

"I imagine so. I'll double-check. But, of course, we want to handle all legal problems for him."

She gave a sigh; my lawyer affects a long-suffering air even when I'm paying her overtime.

"And Lauren Emby. Please call him over at Legal Aid. I want to get in touch with him about our client."

"Emby, in Legal Aid."

"Right. Actually, Martha can handle that if you'll pass on the message. They're being a bit restrictive right now with my phone calls."

"You're in custody?" she said.

"Sort of. The La Perfecta Motel is making unhappy noises. But once our client makes a statement..."

"I think I'd like to speak to your legal adviser on the ground," she said.

"Deirdre, it's me, Anna. You sound as if you're doing a briefing for the State Department."

"I'm thinking quite seriously of government service," she said. I handed her over to the pinup cowboy and they exchanged heavyweight legal jargon to what seemed their entire satisfaction. Three hours later, Mike and I were back on the streets and heading for the hospital, where the word was that Tony Skane was on the top floor with mild concussion and a broken leg. Father Herman was in the trauma unit with third-degree burns on one arm and any number of lesser injuries. He was incommunicado but expected to make a good recovery.

In the best room available, we found a very pale Tony Skane sitting up in bed, with Maria beside him, feeding him Jell-O cubes.

"How are you doing?" I asked.

"All right, considering everything."

"We should not have left him," Maria said severely to me.

"That was my idea entirely," I admitted.

"I jumped out of the truck right behind you," Tony said. "The blast came and I wound up in the road. They must have thought I was dead. Then the farm truck came along and didn't stop quite in time."

"You got a smashed leg, and the colonel and his buddy took off after us?"

"Yes. It really was just as well they were distracted," he told Maria. "The trucker had a CB and called for help. Maybe you could get his name for me."

"I can probably do that." I didn't feel the need to mention that I was in abnormally close contact with both the local and the Arizona State Police.

While Mike had a few quiet words in Spanish with Maria, Tony and I discussed the accident and its aftermath. We did not touch on the main item of outstanding business: the arson case. The doctor had warned me that Tony was suffering from shock; emotional topics were to be strictly avoided.

After our hospital visit, I got on the phone and made plane reservations for the morning, then Mike and I had a meal featuring a great many peppers and spices, which he assured me was ideal for shock in a hot climate. I topped mine off with a straight whiskey, which had significantly more effect.

"Of course she's innocent," he said as we were finishing a chili-laced chicken concoction.

"I think so. We may be able to prove it, too." Maria's revised statement had given me a lot to think about; waiting for busy interns and tetanus shots had provided the time.

"She should have blamed the colonel," Mike said reflectively. "If she had fingered him, I think Skane would have gone along in a minute."

I wasn't so sure of that and said so.

"We talked, you know, at the hospital." His face was still. It struck me that I had never seen Mike look so relaxed.

"The colonel murdered her father. She watched him burn to death."

"I didn't know that. It explains a lot—if we can believe her."

"I believe her," said Mike. "The colonel had his ways."

I didn't say anything.

"I could and *should* have disarmed him." He looked at me, and I reluctantly nodded. Though Mike is an expert at unarmed combat, he is not a particularly good marksman. "You were lucky," he added. "That was a tricky shot under the circumstances. Did you know that?"

The explosion was still ringing in my ears and I was afraid that the red plume and the sudden creeping dark mess were waiting in some other psychic chamber. "Yes," I said. "We're all square now for your good work in the reserve, Mike."

He gave a tight little smile. "That's what I thought. You've always been very fair, Anna."

WE FLEW INTO D.C. early the next afternoon. Harry was there to meet us, and Skipper Norris came along to drive my car, as my hands were still bandaged. The news, which Harry described as sensational and omnipresent, was that Joe Skane had mysteriously disappeared and his chauffeur had decamped. Skane's Mercedes was subsequently found in a parking lot at JFK; opinion on his fate was divided. One faction thought he was in South America; the other, that he slept in the Potomac.

Mike Garrett and Skipper were disappointed; Harry, I could tell, was secretly relieved. I kept my own counsel through a late lunch; after we'd returned to the office and Harry was back at work in his studio, I called a cab. It's a mistake in this business to rely too much on personalities. I'd liked Maria and so I was inclined to think her innocent. Fortunately, the facts seemed to agree. I'd disliked the bossy and vulgar Joe Skane and I would just as soon have proved him a murderer—or at least an accessory. But my desires were quite irrelevant. Joe Skane had a solid alibi, and while the detestable Charlie Ruiz, aka Colonel Garcia, had a broad homicidal streak, he obviously preferred to kill for, rather than against, his interests. Antonia Ceasario might have been an indulgence, a throwback to an earlier life and earlier pleasures, but it had certainly encouraged Luisa's—and Maria's—silence. Helena Skane's death would have been completely counterproductive.

Sad to say, I couldn't see either the colonel or Joe Skane as the arsonist, but that conclusion led me to consider who else might have welcomed Helena Skane's sudden death. Another possibility had been in the back of my mind since I'd heard Maria's revised statement, and when the taxi appeared, I gave the driver Natalie Welsung's Georgetown address.

Chez Welsung proved to be a handsome brick building with white stone trim and shiny green shutters. I had the cabbie drive past and let me out a block away in case the press had staked the place out, but apparently Skane's associates were keeping some of his secrets. Ms. Welsung's home was undisturbed, and when I rang the bell and identified myself, a statuesque gray-haired woman showed me into a little sitting room with a choice collection of Tiffany lamps and French gilt furniture.

Ms. Welsung did not keep me waiting long. Our interview was conducted in a brisk and businesslike fashion. I heard her high heels tapping along the tiled hallway, then the door opened, and a striking woman in a tailored silk suit appeared. Natalie Welsung had dark red hair, large and prominent green eyes, and the unnaturally smooth temples and taut chin of the prematurely face-lifted, but what was really distinctive was the psychic charge that accompanied her. She was like a megavolt Leiden jar, full of spontaneous, and probably noisy, energy.

"You are?" She said in an imperial interrogative.

"Anna Peters, Executive Security. I'm making some inquiries for Maria Rivas's defense counsel, Ms. Welsung, and now that Joseph Skane has disappeared—"

Her flaming red lips contracted to a mean, stubborn line. "Don't speak to me about that filthy bitch!" was her opening, and she went on from there. Natalie Welsung had a creative line in invective and it was powered by pure rage. When I stood up in an effort to stem the flow, she ordered me off her premises then and forever.

"I'm not a journalist," I began, but she turned smartly on her heel and shouted, "Irena! Call the police."

I could see that Ms. Welsung was nothing if not decisive, and I made my exit with as much dignity as I could manage.

"I have nothing to say to anyone," she repeated in an angry contralto. "I have absolutely no information whatsoever about Joe Skane."

Though I was disinclined to believe that, I had already gotten what I'd come for. The house had only a faint, suggestive odor of flowers, but Natalie Welsung was wearing an intense, concentrated scent of gardenias.

ALTHOUGH THE SKANE development's Brae Burn Golf Club was hardly Gleneagles, it certainly wasn't dinky, either, Sabrina Bach to the contrary. The course had well-manicured fairways and velvet greens and the stone-faced clubhouse wore the air of undemanding luxury appropriate for so costly an amenity. The friendly staff were helpful to a prospective member, telling me that Natalie Welsung, who had recommended the course to me so highly, had belonged for just over a year and a half. She often brought friends for tennis and golf and occasionally for swimming. I said I'd like to talk to the resident professional and was directed to the pro shop, which featured nice bright knit shirts, pink-and-yellow-handled graphite tennis rackets, and a bewildering assortment of golf clubs, golf bags, and golf shoes.

My real interest was the row of golf carts lined up alongside the building, but I feigned an attraction for a set of fuzzy animal club covers until the other customers were finished and the club pro came over to see whether I needed help. He had the bluff good nature and permanent reddish tan of those who toil in outdoor recreation and seemed all too willing to lead me down the primrose path of amateur golf.

I introduced myself, took out my identification, and handed it over.

"What's this all about?"

"I notice that you have a lot of golf carts. Could I ask how they are secured at night?"

"In good weather, they're left outside; if it looks like rain, we drive them down to a shed we have. I'm afraid you can't sell us on any more security," he said with a genial laugh. "We almost never have trouble in this neighborhood."

"Not even kids joyriding?"

"No keys, no ride," he said cheerfully, then stopped.

"Yes?"

"We did have one incident. Someone must have left a key in a cart, because we had one driven over a couple of the outer greens."

"When was that?"

"Couple of months ago. Why?"

I explained that I was investigating the Skane arson and that we had reason to believe that the perpetrator had arrived by golf cart.

"The police haven't been to see us," he said doubtfully.

"The Skanes had several golf carts and by the time the emergency vehicles and the fire trucks were finished, I imagine any tracks were pretty well erased. I'm interested in a cart coming from this side of the property."

He thought about this and went outside to the greens-keeper's shed. A moment later, he came back with a thin African-American man with thick glasses and sad, intelligent eyes. "Henri says it was the night of June twenty-sixth. He remembers because he had to work to get the damaged greens ready for the Ladies Members Plate competition that started the twenty-eighth."

"Could you show me which greens were damaged?"

"We'd need to take a cart," Henri said. "The eighth and tenth greens are at the far end of the course."

"Take Ms. Peters down and show her," the pro said, producing a key. "Is that all you need?"

I took out one of my cards and wrote Natalie Welsung's name on it. "I need to know if this member played shortly before the twenty-sixth and whether or not she rented a cart.''

"I'll check the starter's book," he said, suddenly looking unhappy, "but I can answer your second question now: She never walked farther than from the cart to the tee.''

Henri and I got into a white cart with a snappy green-and-white awning and rolled down the wide fairways, passing toiling twosomes and threesomes and scattering the Canada geese that were grazing on the turf like sheep. Henri described his tribulations with these noble but unsanitary birds until we reached the eighth hole, right at the turn of the course. He stopped and pointed to where the cart had cut into the turf to the left of the pin.

"No damage to the fairway, though?''

"No. The weather was dry then, very dry. The fairways were hard, and anyway, golf carts run on them all the time.''

"So it wasn't a kid deliberately trying to cut up the course?''

"No," he agreed with a thoughtful expression. "No, I thought we were just lucky. We were preparing for the tournament and, with the dry weather, I had been watering that day. The greens were wet; the cart sank right in.''

"But just those two greens damaged?''

"Right, and just one track on each. Like somebody drove right over them.''

"Where to? That's the question.''

"From here to the tenth," Henri said, pointing across the fairways.

When we reached the tenth green, we had to wait until a party finished putting. Henri parked the cart near the eleventh tee and gestured back diagonally across the green.

"Straight across?"

"That's right. We had to move the pin for the Ladies Plate and some of the ladies were sure unhappy."

"Do you know whose property adjoins this hole?"

"That's the Skane residence, but we never see them on the course. They're Long Hills people. Between you and me, I think their greens are overrated."

We discussed the relative merits of Long Hills and Brae Burn on the ride back along a little gravel road that just skirted the fairways. Henri was of the opinion that a similar service road would have been a good idea on the outward side of the course. I could see his point, but from my perspective, his damaged greens were an absolute gift.

I got another one when I returned to the pro shop: Natalie Welsung had played golf and rented a cart three days before the fire. "Her first visit for some time," the pro said. He had brightened up when he'd found she had not been there the twenty-fifth or the twenty-sixth, and I decided he was not a man with much imagination.

"The cart, could you tell which one had been out?"

"Sure could. It was muddy from tearing across the greens for one thing and one of the tires was chewed up. In fact, we had to get it repainted, too."

"Would you have reported that to the police by any chance?"

"Well, not that they could do anything about it, you know, but to satisfy the insurance..."

"They assumed a key had been left in the machine?"

"What else? Though I'm careful and Henri helps me check them every night. You can always slip up, though."

"Was there a key in it when it was returned?"

"No, and that was the funny thing. We found the key later just where it should have been."

I shook his hand gratefully. "You've been more help than you can possibly imagine," I said.

SEVENTEEN

THE FUNNY THING about clients is that you never quite know how they're going to react to success. That goes ditto for police, and even for family. Instead of being thrilled and delighted to have a whole new approach to the Skane arson, the District's finest made heavy weather about the contradictions and delays in Maria's statement. To be fair, they finally got themselves in gear and visited Natalie Welsung just as that tempestuous person was packing for a flight to Caracas.

I missed the resulting conflagration, which was only dampened when the officers discovered a golf cart's ignition key still on her key ring. Eventually, they located the D.C. locksmith who had made a key for her from a wax impression; Ms. Welsung was not only tempestuous but also determined and resourceful.

At this point, Lauren Emby abandoned his defeatist thoughts of plea bargaining and filed for dismissal of all charges. His picture on the front page of the *Post* was elegant enough for *Gentleman's Quarterly*. Unlike most of the others connected with the case, Lauren Emby was happy with me, and I intend to speak well of him now and in the future.

My clients were less pleased. Amend that: Tony was ecstatic, or as ecstatic as one can be with a broken leg and a plaster cast in sticky D.C. weather. Maria was another matter. She did not contact me after Emby had given her the good news. She did not return my calls, either. In fact, I ran into her only by accident—at a gas station, of all places. I had just filled my car when a scooter pulled in behind me. I turned around and saw Maria removing a shiny black helmet.

She took a deep breath and said, "You have ruined my life."

I thought that was a little much. "I beg your pardon. Last time I noticed, you'd been charged with arson-murder and were being pursued by a psychopathic ex-Guatemalan army colonel."

She flicked her hand to indicate the irrelevance of those tribulations. "She will be put on trial."

"Natalie Welsung? You bet she will."

"They will ask her why she did it. And she will tell them that Joe Skane wished to leave her."

"Ah," I said. Sometimes the oldest of old stories turns out to be the correct one. "He wanted to leave her for you?"

"It was not my wish," she said quickly, twisting her hands together in distress. "He discovered my *abuela,* my grandmother, the one I visited on the *moto.* Tony thinks she's overstayed her visa."

"You were concerned there might be trouble with Immigration?"

"She could not be sent back!" Maria exclaimed. "She would have been killed. You do not understand. My grandfather was a labor leader. He was murdered for printing union leaflets. Grandmother stayed on because of my father. When my father was murdered, she was desperate to leave. What could I do? Your government would not give her asylum. I borrowed money from the señor and got her into the country.''

''From Señor Skane.''

She nodded.

''And later he found out you'd broken the law and brought your grandmother in?''

''It cannot be illegal to protect an old woman with a broken heart,'' Maria said passionately.

''It cannot be wrong,'' I said, ''but it certainly is illegal.'' I thought I could see the whole scenario. ''And so Señor Skane blackmailed you.''

She looked puzzled.

''He knew about your grandmother and so you were in his power?''

She shrugged. ''One lives as one can.''

''Yes, I understand that.'' And I did. Our lives had a kind of inverted symmetry. The combination of power and poverty that had once led me to crime had led her to vice.

''Then Tony came back from the Southwest and we fell in love. He doesn't know,'' she said in anguish. ''He doesn't know anything.''

''He must be told,'' I said. ''It will be easier if he is told now.''

''You don't understand. Tony has always been rich. He has never been desperate,'' she said. ''I wish you had left me in jail!''

I felt sorry for her, but I could not help being angry, too. ''Don't be melodramatic and childish,'' I said. ''Would you rather Tony had seen the woman he loves executed for murdering his mother? Would you rather have him believe his father contracted his mother's death? He can't be protected forever, but those lies would have been crueler than the truth."

"But I cannot live with that truth," she said, and without bothering to fill her tank, she jumped on the scooter and sped away.

A COLD RAIN ran down the windows, drenching impartially the protesters in Lafayette Park, the tourists on the Mall, and the bureaucrats scattered from the Hill to Foggy Bottom. We had somehow leapt straight from mid-summer to late fall; and the long days of humid heat had transformed themselves to a chilly downpour that was turning the usual urban detritus to mush. Though it was barely three o'clock, the sky was already darkening when I heard the phone ring in the outer office. A moment later, Martha buzzed through to me. "It's Mr. Smith again," she said. "He's at that burger shop on the corner. He wants to know if you're free."

"Tell him to come on over. I'll meet him downstairs."

Five minutes later, Tony swung into the foyer on his crutches. He had just a sweater, no raincoat, no hat, no umbrella; he was soaked to the skin.

"You better come into the studio," I said. "My husband keeps a lot of old sweatshirts around to work in."

"I called you on impulse." His face was thinner. He looked as if he had aged and joined the grown-ups in a matter of weeks. To my taste, that suited him.

"So I see. In here." I opened the door to the workshop area and waved to Billy, Harry's assistant, who was busy with one of the presses.

"This doesn't look much like a detective agency."

"This is Helios Workshop. Executive Security is upstairs." I checked the row of hooks alongside the entry. "How about this one with coordinating magenta ink stains? A Harry Radford original."

"Maybe I'd better." Tony pulled off his sodden sweater. The striped shirt underneath was blotched with damp. He took that off as well and pulled on the frayed navy sweatshirt.

"We can go upstairs or we can talk here," I told him. "Harry's off setting up an exhibition today, and we won't bother Billy. He's quite deaf."

"I think I'd rather talk here. It's not really detective business." He looked at some of the proofs that were pinned up on the wall. The illustrations for the Lem novel were complex; if I understood Harry's technical explanations correctly, an aquatint had been overprinted by a second etched plate. The result was a double image, the voluptuous and beautiful world the characters in the novel secured through drugs, the impoverished and ugly reality that their pharmaceuticals concealed.

"*The Futurological Congress,*" I said, "a novel by the Polish science fiction writer Stanislaw Lem. A peculiar genius."

"Beauty as illusion," Tony remarked. "An update of *Death and the Maiden.*"

"Something like that. But those are the two extremes, aren't they?"

"What do you mean?"

"Most of us exist somewhere in the middle, between the true and beautiful on one side and the false and ugly on the other."

"I don't care," he said abruptly. "I was upset, but I really don't care what was between her and my father."

"She wished to protect you," I said carefully. "And maybe to protect your idea of her, too."

"She lied to protect her grandmother, she lied to protect my father; and she lied to protect me."

"Mike Garrett tells me she watched her father burned alive when a death squad set their print shop on fire. I imagine that would make one protective. I imagine nothing else would seem too terrible, not even prison."

"She's gone," he said.

"Is she with her grandmother?"

Tony shook his head.

"Does the old lady know where she is?"

"I'm not sure."

"I see. Are you asking me to find her?"

Tony did not reply and seemed absorbed in Harry's detailed and grotesquely beautiful prints.

"I don't think she will have returned to Guatemala."

He shook his head.

"Luisa? Would she be with Luisa?"

"I've checked that," he said.

"I would call Father Herman," I said.

"He won't say, but I think that is where she is."

"Then don't be a fool. If you love her and nothing
else matters, get on a plane today."

I think that is what he had come to hear, because he
suddenly demanded, "Do you think it could work
out?"

I hesitated. I am paid, after all, to deliver facts and
figures, dates and times and probable causes. Matters
of the heart are extracurricular, so to speak. "I think
you need to make a romantic gesture," I said. "I think
you need to pursue her without any guarantee."

"Yes," he said. "Yes, I think that's right." He
turned and hobbled out the door and into the foyer.
Through the window, I could see that it was raining
harder than ever.

"Maybe I should call you a cab," I suggested.

"Make it an airport cab," he said with an air of decision. "There'll be a Tucson flight sooner or later."

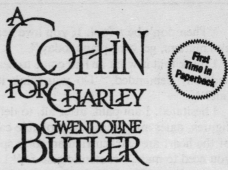

First Time in Paperback

A COFFIN FOR CHARLEY
GWENDOLINE BUTLER

An Inspector John Coffin Mystery

IT'S HOT...AND GETTING HOTTER FOR COMMANDER JOHN COFFIN

His wife, actress Stella Pinero, is being stalked. Adding to his worries, London's Second City is terrified by a cunning and inventive serial killer. Coffin has cast a wide net, but the killer is elusive...and continuing to kill.

Somehow connected is a murder that occurred twenty years before. A young girl had witnessed the crime and testified. Now the killers are free and returning home, possibly for revenge. When Coffin's niece turns up missing, he fears the worst—pushing himself and his force into London's darkest underbelly to match skill and cunning with crime's cleverest own....

"Butler excels..."   —*Publishers Weekly*

Available in May at your favorite retail stores.

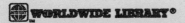 **WORLDWIDE LIBRARY®**   CHARLEY

ALASKA GRAY

First Time in Paperback

SUSAN FROETSCHEL

A Jane McBride Mystery

NEW BEGINNINGS, DEADLY ENDINGS

Jane McBride is a woman with secrets and sadness—and
Alaska seems just about as far away as she can get from
her past.

Her big welcome comes in the form of an anonymous
phone call telling her to leave. Then Jane learns that the
finance job she left Boston for has been eliminated. But the
beauty of Sitka lures her, and she is determined to stay—
even after she surprises an intruder ransacking her room.

The death of a young local woman has no connection to
her...or does it? Soon Jane is trapped in the middle of a
very sophisticated evil in the small town....

"A page-turner..."—*Pittsburgh Advertiser*

Available in July at your favorite retail stores.

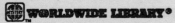

GRIZZLY

CHRISTINE ANDREAE

A Lee Squires Mystery

FAIR GAME

English professor Lee Squires is spending Easter break in Montana as cook for the J-E dude ranch, where friend and owner Dave Fife is hoping that some Japanese investors—plied with home cooking—will pour cash into the struggling J-E.

Lee has come ready to whip up hotcakes, biscuits and chicken fried steak—but not to wrestle her libido over Dave's brother, Mac, a tireless bear activist...or to find a dead body with missing parts.

Another mangled body later, officials are hunting a bear. Lee doesn't buy the theory—but in tracking the truth, she comes face-to-face with a human killer who is nothing short of...grizzly.

"Good character interaction, great sense of place, and steady suspense." —*Library Journal*

Available in May at your favorite retail stores.

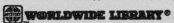